the Resilient One

Cami Checketts

Birch River Publishing
Smithfield, Utah
Published in the United States of America
Cover design: Christina Dymock
Interior design: Heather Justesen
Editing: Daniel Coleman

the Resilient One

Birch River Publishing
Smithfield Utah

Cami Checketts

Dedication

To my sweetheart of a friend, Jeanette Lewis. Thank you for including me in The Billionaire Bride Pact and for being such a wonderful example of an amazing mother, writer, and friend.

Introduction by Lucy McConnell

I've heard it said that some people come into your life and quickly leave—others leave footprints on your heart. Jeanette and Cami are two wonderful authors and women who have left their mark on my heart. Their overwhelming support, knowledge, and general goodness have pushed me forward as a writer and nurtured me as a friend. That's why I'm pleased to introduce you to their new and innovative series: The Billionaire Bride Pact Romances.

In each story, you'll find romance and character growth. I almost wrote personal growth—forgetting these are works of fiction—because the books we read become a part of us, their words stamped into our souls. As with any good book, I disappeared into the pages for a while and was able to walk sandy beaches, visit a glass blowing shop, and spend time with a group of women who had made a pact—a pact that influenced their lives, their loves, and their dreams.

I encourage you to put your feet up, grab a cup of something wonderful, and fall in love with a billionaire today.

Wishing you all the best,
Lucy McConnell
Author of *The Professional Bride*

The Billionaire Bride Pact

I, Alyssa Armsworth, do solemnly swear that someday I will marry a billionaire and live happily ever after. If I fail to meet my pledge, I will stand up at my wedding reception and sing the Camp Wallakee theme song.

Chapter One

Alyssa's uneven gait pounded through the miles as she enjoyed the running path along Ka'anapali Beach. She had to cut away from the water line and up to the road because of the rocky shoreline next to the Hilton, but within half a mile she could see the ocean again. Life was just better when she could see the ocean.

A loud trumpet blasted through her earbuds. Alyssa jumped. Her heart hammered as she forced her legs out of their rhythm and slowed to a walk. She pulled her earbuds out and retrieved the phone from the pouch in her running pants, cursing her best friend, Maryn, for putting the annoying trumpet as her ringtone and cursing herself for not changing it.

"Why haven't you answered my calls?"

"Sprinting makes the palms a bit slick." Better not to admit she didn't answer last night because she was editing photos and didn't want to be interrupted.

"Well, stop sprinting and answer the blasted phone." Maryn huffed. "*The* best friend should have priority over everything else. You know I'm just jealous because you can outrun me even with your nubbin of a foot, but it always stresses me out when you sprint. What if you fell?"

Alyssa stopped, breathing deeply and focusing on the picturesque Airport Beach, loving the taste of salt in the air. The water lapped onto the beige sand from an ocean as dark blue as midnight. She loved Maui early in the morning in January. The weather was beautiful as always, but the tourists were scarce. She leaned forward to stretch tight hamstrings. Her dark ponytail fell over her shoulder and obscured the view. She pushed it away. She wasn't offended by Maryn's reference to her misshapen foot. It did make running more difficult, but she wasn't going to let a deformity she'd dealt with since birth dictate her life.

"You do realize it's six a.m.?" Alyssa asked. Maryn usually wasn't an early riser, unless she had inspiration to write an article on a celebrity or some other sensational story that would make her money. Six a.m. in Maui would mean eight a.m. in Los Angeles. Still too early for her night owl of a friend.

"Who cares? I need a favor."

"No. You?" Alyssa hoped she laid the sarcasm on thick enough. Maryn was forever in need of favors to boost her freelance career. It used to work well when Alyssa was developing her portfolio as a photographer, but her brand of capturing candid human interaction had taken off and she was now sold in studios throughout America as well as a prosperous internet business. "I'm not taking any pictures of celebrities for scum-bag magazines." It was humiliating that she'd ever done that for Maryn, but it had paid the bills when they were living on Top Ramen and showering at the local recreation center because their utilities were shut off.

"No. I'm way past that. This new magazine is on the up and up."

Alyssa hoped that was true. Maryn worked for so many different magazines it was difficult to know which were smut and which were respectable. Alyssa started walking the beach trail. Might as well get in more mileage, even if it was at a slower pace. With the special orthotics in her shoe, she barely limped. Thank heavens for modern medicine.

"So…" Maryn continued when Alyssa didn't reply. "All I need you to do is meet a guy and get him to ask you out."

"*What?*" Alyssa stopped walking again.

"Hey, I understand the life of a recluse is oh so appealing and good-looking men are oh so scary, but this is going to be easy as a chocolate truffle. He's filthy rich, hot, and he's coming to you. Plus, if you land him you could be number three of the twelve to keep The Pact. Can't wait to trap my own hot Richie." Maryn laughed, obviously pleased with herself, but Alyssa knew her friend would never marry a wealthy man. She had too many issues from being half-starved most of her life.

"I am so confused right now." Alyssa tried to breathe slowly and watch the waves to bring some sense of calm. She did not need to be reminded of a pact she should never have made at girl's camp when she was too young and stupid to understand the influence of peer pressure. A pact she had no desire to fulfill. Her dad had pushed plenty of "Richies" on her and she would never consent to being sold to the highest bidder. She focused back on her friend. How exactly was Maryn arranging for some billionaire to come to her?

"Thanks to Nikki, Holly, and Taylor's exclusive interviews, and Erin's ideas for how to sniff out the men with money, my article on how to pick up billionaires went viral." Maryn squealed happily. "Of course I didn't share that Taylor is already divorced, would've put a damper on the situation. Now I've got several magazines begging me for a follow-up so I thought, hey, let's do something on how to meet those reclusive Richies. The humble, sweet ones that everyone wants to get their hands on."

It was much too easy to imagine Maryn rubbing her hands together in anticipation.

"I'm happy for Nikki and Holly, but honestly they can keep their billionaire husbands." Nikki had been the picture of bridal bliss at her wedding a couple of months ago. Holly on the other hand didn't look thrilled with life. Hopefully she was happy. "But remember,"

Alyssa said to Maryn. "I'm the 'prude'. I'll never marry a rich man." She was perfectly content with her career and no man controlling her like her father had attempted to do.

"Would you forget about that jerk? I swear, if I could cut his parts off I would. You are not a prude just because you wouldn't give Hugh what he wanted. That man thought he was Hugh Hefner and you were a Playboy Bunny. Nasty a-hole!"

Alyssa winced. She shouldn't have said anything that brought Hugh into the conversation. It never failed to rile Maryn. A cool breeze made her shiver. "So how am I supposed to help you with your article?" Alyssa asked, more than ready to forget about Hugh.

"The magazine gave me a few leads and when I got the portfolio on this one, I knew, he was *your* guy."

"My guy?" Sweat dripped down her back and Alyssa was afraid very little of it had to do with the physical exertion of a few minutes ago.

"Don't interrupt. He loves photography, children, and charity. Ka-bam. He's like your soul mate."

"Ka-bam?" Alyssa exhaled slowly. "He's probably lying that he loves those things to make himself look good for the press." She lifted her long hair and fanned her neck.

"Stop stereotyping! Not everyone is like that cheesy politician you dated. What was his name, Joe?"

"Joel." Okay, maybe she was being stereotypical but that was exactly what her father and his cronies used to do and probably still did. Joel and Hugh were some of the worst. Pretending to be charitable and really only caring about how to take advantage of others.

"Forget about Joel. The hottie Beckham is flying into Maui today. I've got his itinerary and one of his stops is your art show and another one is that children's center you love to visit. He'll be there for over a week. All you have to do is flirt a bit, get him to ask you out, and then tell me about it. You're perfect—the classy and beautiful type that every rich guy would be drawn to, plus no man can resist your ethnic flare. Ooh, if I just had that olive skin!" Maryn paused for a breath but Alyssa didn't feel the need to counter-compliment. Maryn was absolutely gorgeous with her petite frame, blonde hair, and blue eyes, and one of the many things Alyssa loved about her best friend was no matter what she claimed, she didn't have a jealous bone in her body.

"It's just a generic article so I won't put names or pictures in it," Maryn continued. "See, Easy-schmeasy-lemon-cheesy. You don't even have to go on the date..." Her voice dropped. "*Unless* you want to."

"I won't want to," Alyssa said too forcefully. She took a long breath, anxiety from the thought of picking up on some rich guy making her a bit light-headed. Why was the name *Beckham* familiar? This had disaster written all over it. "This seems too easy for one of your favors. Why would your editor be interested in a generic article about me getting asked on one date?"

"It's part of a bigger plan. No worries. Will you do it? Please, please, please?"

"So I don't have to go out with him, just get him to ask and give him the wrong number?"

"For sure. Great idea."

Alyssa looked out at the water. She didn't want to date some wealthy schmoozer. Someday she'd love to find someone who cared for children as much as she did and would be happy taking her on a hike instead of insisting she be his arm candy at some exclusive event. She didn't need a man trying to buy her affection. Her father's love language was all dollars, deposits, and dividends—and she used the term "father" in the loosest possible way.

"Hello? Are you still there?" Maryn called out. "Come on Ally. You love me and I need your help."

How could she turn down one of the two people who had always been there for her? Maryn had been her friend their entire lives. Maryn's mom had been a maid for Alyssa's dad from the time Maryn was two. Alyssa's dad had liked the feisty Maryn so he'd always treated her like a second daughter and paid for both of them to go to girl's camp or whatever else they begged him for. When they hit teenage years it all changed and they both realized her dad was nothing more than a blackmailing predator, intent on using both of them in whatever way would make him money or make him look good to his friends.

The two girls had moved an hour north of Newport Beach to L.A. breaking away her dad's influence, and pursuing their dreams with college and then with fledgling careers. A majority of the time, they'd only kept the utilities on because of Alyssa's photography and Maryn's nose for finding writing opportunities. If it hadn't been for Alyssa's Granny Ellie sneaking money to Maryn every chance she could, they would've been forced to the food pantry.

"Okay." She heard herself concede and sighed.

"Yes! Oh, yeah, that's my girl." Maryn sang out. Alyssa knew the happy dance was in full swing. "I'll send you his picture and all the information for how to snare him."

"*Snare* him?"

"I mean the places he'll be the next week in case you don't get a date offer from the gallery meeting."

"It's getting heavy," Alyssa sighed.

"No, no heaviness, all good things, light things, think cotton candy, pink cotton candy." Now Maryn would be flinging her hands in lightening gestures. "Email me everything after you meet him and then you're off the hook."

"You owe me."

"I know, but you never ask for repays so I just keep smiling all the way to success."

"You do that." Alyssa hit the end button and shoved the phone back in her pocket. She turned around and retraced her route toward Lahaina and the bed and breakfast where she had taken up semi-permanent residence. Alyssa had moved to Maui to escape her father over a month ago. Even though Alyssa would never consent to live with her parents in their Newport Beach mansion, her dad never quit trying to keep tabs on her. She didn't know when or if she was going back to California and face that family nightmare.

Had she really just agreed to stalk a man until he asked her out? She'd done worse things for Maryn, but this one made her stomach pitch as if she was on a whale-watching tour on stormy seas. Every detail was like a whale's blowhole spraying rank water at her. At least she didn't really have to go on the date. Maybe he wouldn't even be interested in her. She'd give it a try for Maryn—smile and act nice. If she got the offer, then she'd give him a wrong phone number, and make herself scarce the week he was here.

Her shoulders relaxed as the plan formulated and her running became rhythmic and comfortable. Everything would be fine. She could help Maryn out and stay away from rich men who always had an agenda that had nothing to do with what was best for anyone but them. Who cared that she'd never fulfill the pact she'd made with her friends at summer camp? Some things were better left in the past and the Billionaire Brides Pact was buried and dead as far as she was concerned.

Her phone chimed. She didn't want to stop, but she couldn't deny herself a quick glimpse at the picture of the man she was supposed to "snare". She slowed to a walk and opened the email from Maryn and then stopped in her tracks for the second time that morning. Her hand flew to her mouth as her stomach dropped.

"Oh, no. Oh, Maryn. What have you got me into this time? This is never going to work."

Chapter Two

Beck kept his sunglasses on as he exited the plane and made his way toward baggage claim. His assistant, Linli, always laughed at him for flying commercial, but he felt guilty splurging on chartered flights. He picked up his rental car and was on his way to the west side of the island without any incident. Linli was convinced someone had hacked her computer and obtained his schedule, but based on the lack of paparazzi at the airport, it looked like she was being hyper-paranoid. As usual.

Beck's shoulders relaxed as the tropical breeze blew through the window. Hopefully he could find the photographer, A. A., and talk him into working with Beck's charity, Jordan's Buds. Linli had tried every avenue to contact A.A. but the guy really liked his privacy. No contact information anywhere.

After Beck found A.A. he could relax and enjoy the island for the week. It had been much too long since he'd traveled and not had a full agenda. Most of his humanitarian trips had him scheduled every hour of daylight—meeting with officials, coaching and encouraging his charity supervisors, digging wells for clean water, building houses or schools, and visiting children. Time with the children made it all worth it, but he was exhausted. Lying by a beach sounded pretty nice right now.

Siri talked him around the south-western side of the island. The ocean view and the sound of waves crashing was exactly the tonic he needed. He drove through Lahaina and instead of stopping at his bed and breakfast to check in, he went to the first public parking lot he could find close to the beach.

Stepping out of the car, he stretched in the early morning sunlight and simply inhaled the salty tang as he listened to the waves. This was going to be a nice vacation. He studied the deep blue of the ocean, but a noisy family unloading their beach paraphernalia interrupted any relaxation for a minute.

Beck watched as the mother of two demanded her children stay close while she proceeded to stack chairs, umbrella, and a small cooler on her husband's waiting arms. She climbed back into the car to retrieve more junk while the man stood patiently waiting to be loaded up. Beck couldn't help but chuckle. The guy didn't look like he was enjoying himself, but Beck still felt a twinge of jealousy. He wanted that... someday.

A movement out of the corner of his eye drew his attention. The tow-headed toddler had somehow escaped her parent's notice as they unloaded their car. The little girl was through the parking lot, halfway across the sand, and headed straight for the water.

"Hey," Beck yelled.

The dad looked at him in confusion. Beck pointed at the child but quickly realized that he was not only closer, he wasn't loaded like a pack mule. Beck took off at a sprint toward the water. The little girl walked unsteadily through the sand as the water receded. A large wave surged up the beach headed straight for the child, sweeping her feet out from under her. She cried out in surprise as she fell on her rear. Twenty more yards. Beck increased his speed but the sand slowed his steps. The little girl sat crying in the sand, unaware of the danger as the water had receded and she didn't see the huge wave rolling toward her. The undercurrent of this wave could take her and nobody would find her again.

"Oomph!" Beck ran straight into a jogger.

The ground came rushing up to meet him. Beck instinctively put his arms around the much smaller runner and curled to the side so he'd take the impact of the hit. The sand was soft and the person small enough, he didn't feel much pain. He skidded to a stop and glanced into the face of the most beautiful woman he'd encountered in a long, long time. For a second he could only stare, unable to remember simple facts, like his own name.

She didn't say anything, just stared at him, her dark eyes filled with shock.

Remembrance came rushing back like the wave that could take the little girl. He released his hold on the woman and rushed out the words, "I'm so sorry. The little girl."

He looked up. The child was face down in the water and the wave was tugging her small frame back into its depths. Her parents were screaming and running for her, but Beck was still closer. He pushed off the ground, ran the final steps, and scooped the toddler up. Her face was covered with wet sand and she was coughing and sputtering for air.

The mother reached him first and snatched her little girl from his arms. The child sucked in a full breath and Beck breathed easier himself. He turned away to look for the woman he'd run into, but the father of the child came rushing up and pumped his hand, thumping him on the back. "Thanks, oh, man. Thanks. Sara. My little girl."

The man continued thanking him and Beck said "you're welcome" and "no problem" until he felt like a recording. He backed away smiling and acknowledging the thanks before spinning to try and glimpse the woman he'd literally ran into. Sadly, she had disappeared.

He debated trying to run after her, but knew he probably wouldn't catch her as he wasn't dressed to run and didn't know if she'd continued along the shoreline or turned up one of the streets of Lahaina. He wandered the beach for a little bit, trying to trace her footprints but there were too many. Plowing into her had all happened so quickly, but the feel of her in his arms and the beauty of her dark eyes wouldn't be something he'd soon forget. He had to see her again, even if just to know if she was as perfect as he remembered. Getting to know her or asking her out was too much to dream of at this point, but he'd do about anything for another glimpse at her face.

After a while, he returned to the spot where he'd seen her. Still no sign that she had ever been there. The little family was all happily playing in the sand, unaware of what Beck had missed out on. Beck climbed back into his car and drove the couple of blocks to the Garden Gate Bed and Breakfast. It wasn't anything fancy, but it looked clean and comfortable, just like he liked. The host, Jerry, greeted him by the breakfast buffet in the outdoor courtyard.

"Just in time for breakfast," the fifty-something man with a large smile and balding head said. His skin was too pale to be a native, but he looked like he'd lived here long enough to be relaxed and always grinning. "Those redeye flights are awful. Let's get you checked into your room and then you can come join us or get some sleep if you're exhausted."

"Thanks, breakfast sounds great." Beck went inside Jerry's office, signed in and verified that the correct credit card was on file then hefted his luggage and followed Jerry back outside and up several flights of exterior stairs.

The same woman from the beach descended the stairs toward them. Beck stuttered back a step. He didn't think he'd ever see her again and this view hit him as hard as when he'd crashed into her on the beach.

She was exotic-looking with long dark hair, olive skin, and

almond-shaped eyes. Beck edged out of the way so she could make it past him and his luggage, hoping his mouth wasn't hanging open. Now that he'd found her, he wanted to talk to her, apologize again for being so careless this morning, but he didn't know quite what to say.

"Good morning, Alyssa," Jerry called out. "How far did you run today?"

"Eight." She smiled, but then she met Beck's gaze. Her smile changed from open to guarded and those dark eyes lost their sparkle. He clutched his luggage handle. Oh, no. She thought he'd just knocked her over on purpose this morning and then run away instead of making a sufficient apology.

"Hi," he offered. "I'm sorry about this morning. A little girl was in trouble in the waves."

"No, it's fine," she replied, but still looked warily at him.

She slipped past him, leaving only a whiff of vanilla in her path. Beck inhaled slowly, turning to watch her go. She was even more beautiful than he'd built up in his mind. Even though she didn't seem interested in him, at least he knew where she was staying and might have a chance of breaking down whatever barriers she'd put up.

She had a slight limp and wore running shoes with a long skirt and fitted t-shirt. Had she hurt herself running this morning? Aw, crap. Had he injured her when he tackled her? His face filled with color and his stomach rolled. He'd hit her hard enough to hurt her leg or foot. No wonder she was looking at him like he'd poisoned her cat.

Jerry reached the top of the stairs and turned back to Beck. Beck forced himself to stop watching the woman. *Alyssa.* Maybe if he hurried he could talk to her at breakfast. He jogged up a few steps, but then slowed. This wasn't like him. The man who tried to keep a low profile and stay away from women who always seemed to only want him for his looks or his money, mostly the latter. Well, Alyssa hadn't seemed interested in his looks and if he was vague enough she might not learn he had money until she got to know him.

Jerry had a smirk on his face when Beck reached his side. "Don't expect to get anywhere with our Alyssa. I've watched her shoot down man after man."

Beck arched his eyebrows. "Thanks for the advice."

"But it doesn't hurt to look, right bro?" Jerry slapped him on the shoulder and laughed.

Beck glanced down from the balcony to the courtyard. Alyssa had a phone to her ear, but she chose that moment to look up. Her mouth softened for a second and he thought she might smile at him, but she frowned instead and turned away.

Didn't hurt to look? It might.

Chapter Three

"Maryn!" Alyssa gulped for air and then rushed out the words, "He ran into me, like knocked me off my feet then cradled me in his arms." Wow, it had felt good to be sheltered like that. It was like Beckham's basic instinct was to shield her from harm. She couldn't recall a man's touch ever being one of protection instead of blatant desire, and for the first time in a long while she'd wanted to stay wrapped in a man's arms. "He was rescuing a little girl, like superhero rescue guy, and he's amazing and good-looking and I am telling you, I can't do this! I just saw him again. He's staying at *my* bed and breakfast." Alyssa paced the small courtyard, grateful no one else was in the courtyard.

"Whoa, slow down. You're sounding like me." Maryn laughed; obviously Alyssa's distress cracked her up. "When did he run into you? What little girl did he save and why on earth would a Richie stay at your dumpy bed and breakfast? That wasn't in the itinerary."

"After I talked to you, I was running back and he literally plowed me over." Alyssa relived the feeling of his huge body surrounding hers. He was so strong she could feel the strength and firmness of his chest through his shirt. "Then he apologized and went and saved a little girl from the ocean."

"Whoa. And you stuck around to tell him what a hero he was?"

"Yeah, right." After making sure the little girl was okay, Alyssa had run away so fast, she didn't know she was capable of breaking the local speed limit.

14

"Oh." Maryn sighed heavily. "A bit of oohing and aahing would've been nice, but, no worries, actually better than no worries about him staying at your spot. This is going to be perfect! You'll have even more access to him."

"Perfect?" she hissed into the phone. "That's the problem. He's too perfect. The pictures you sent don't do him justice."

"He doesn't like to be photographed, so they never get great pics of him. Glad to hear he's even finer in person."

"I can't believe you don't remember... Beckham Taylor." For such a smart woman, Maryn could be forgetful sometimes. "I photographed him! For you and one of your stupid tabloids."

"What? No!" Maryn gasped.

"His family had some kind of tragedy." Her mind was scrambling to remember all the details, but she couldn't forget the sad look in his eyes when she'd taken those photographs a few years ago.

She could hear Maryn flipping through papers. She loved to have tangible evidence of everything and had filing cabinets full. "Yes. I remember now. Give me a second." More shuffling. "Oh, crap, here it is. He was a huge star in the NHL before his parents died in a car wreck and he inherited millions and not just a couple millions, loads of millions. He quit hockey to focus on managing all their real estate and Jordan's Buds, it's a huge charity for impoverished children throughout the world. Wowza. So you remember taking his picture?"

"Yes, as he left the funeral, and you sold them with an article about him and his family. The magazine twisted the pictures to make it look like he and his sister were fighting when really he was comforting her and helping her with her son."

"Okay, that's bad, but he'll never find out it was you. Even if he remembers the article, which I doubt as there were probably dozens of articles about him and their family circulating then, he won't remember who the photographer was."

Alyssa shook her head. "This isn't going to work, Maryn. Even if I hadn't sold those photos." She could picture it now. Him hugging his sister as they left the cemetery. The magazine may have convinced America that his family was being ripped apart because Beck was the one in control of his parent's money, but Alyssa knew how tender he'd been with his sister and his nephew. She hadn't been immune to his appeal then or now, but she'd forced herself not to think about it. Even though the story looked bad, she'd heard how women still flocked to him. As good-looking and wealthy as he was, he obviously had no problem with flockage.

"You know me. I don't do well with wealthy, hot guys," Alyssa said. "They're always jerks once you get to know them."

"He's not a jerk. I promise. He is fully committed to helping children. He's a great guy. I've really checked him out. I mean, not just his looks, his character and all that crap that matters to you."

"You're sure?" She twisted a lock of hair on her finger.

"I promise you, Alyssa, this is the guy for…" Maryn's voice trailed off. "He's a super-nice guy. Don't shut yourself off before you even talk to him. Be nice to him and get that date offer."

Alyssa turned and Beckham Taylor stood at the bottom of the stairs on the other side of the courtyard, watching her like she was a cat who might leap and scratch his eyes out any minute. She sighed. This was going to be harder than Maryn could understand. She forced some gaiety into her voice. "Sounds great. I'll talk to you later."

"He's right there? Oooh," Maryn squealed. "This is going to be sweet. Ta-ta."

Alyssa restrained from rolling her eyes and dropped her phone into her purse. She took a deep breath and tried to release the tension in her shoulders. He was still watching her. Go on the offensive and introduce herself? Tell him how amazing he was rescuing the little girl this morning? Or head for the food and hope he came to her? She glanced at his slightly-mussed dark hair and the hopeful expression in his impossibly blue eyes. His jaw line was firm, just like she liked, and from his build she could tell he'd probably been a fabulous hockey player. She darted toward the food. What a wimp.

Piling her plate with papaya, boiled eggs, and a bagel, she grabbed some POG juice and sat at one of the tables. Of course today would be the day the breakfast wasn't busy. Only her and some famous, hot, rich man. Where was Jerry? Where was the cute elderly couple, Simon and Kendra, who always told her about their Maui adventures every morning? Maryn was exaggerating, this bed and breakfast wasn't a dump, but still why would a super wealthy dude stay at one of the least expensive places on the west side of the island?

Beckham helped himself to food while she started eating. She tried not to watch him out of the corner of her eye. It was impossible not to look when he marched straight up to her table. "Is this seat taken?"

"All the other tables are full?"

His welcoming smile faded. He looked like she'd just busted his Lego creation.

"I'm just teasing. Please." She gestured toward the seat. He settled his food on the bamboo table. As his juice tipped precariously to the side, they both reached out to steady it. His hand came around hers. The warmth of his rough fingers sent tremors up her arm. Their eyes met and neither of them moved. Awkwardness settled in quickly. "If you'll let go, I can put your juice in a safer spot."

He nodded but didn't move his hand. "What if I don't want to let go?"

She moved her hand quickly and he barely caught the juice before it spilt. Studying her plate, Alyssa forced herself to peel a boiled egg and hoped he couldn't see how he was making her shake. Maryn was so dead.

"I apologize again about this morning. Did I hurt you?" His eyes lowered to her legs and she knew he'd noticed her limp.

"No. You did a great job of protecting me with your body." Her face flamed red and she took a quick drink of her juice.

A slow grin appeared on Beck's face. "I'm glad you're okay."

She nodded her acknowledgment, her stomach fluttering like it was full of fireflies. Oh, my, he looked good when he smiled like that. They ate in silence for several minutes. Alyssa didn't know what to say to break the awkwardness that settled in again.

"So, um, I hear you're a Maui veteran." He forked a bite of eggs, sneaking a glance at her then focusing on his food.

"Where did you hear that from?" Alyssa realized there was too much bite in her voice. She couldn't be herself around handsome, wealthy men. Maryn was going to have to find someone else to quote for her article and just deal with disappointment, Alyssa couldn't handle this.

Beckham's eyes widened and she was caught off guard studying the brightness of the blue. Caribbean blue, sky blue, or maybe almost aqua blue? She couldn't quite decide and she couldn't tear her gaze away from his. What she wouldn't give to photograph him, for her private collection this time.

"Jerry," he said.

"Oh." She spread cream cheese on her bagel, wondering if the air was really crackling around them or if she was going nuts. He had this draw that was so exciting she wanted to either snuggle up next to him or hide in her room.

Beckham set his fork down and cleared his throat. "I don't have anything planned the next couple of days. Would you be interested in... showing me around?"

Alyssa hated that she wondered if this would qualify as him asking her on a date. She wanted to meet his eyes and get lost in the blue again, but she just couldn't do it. What if he was like Hugh? She couldn't be alone with a man and risk being vulnerable. If she couldn't escape from a wiry guy like Hugh how could she protect herself from someone built like Beckham? She could still feel Hugh's manicured fingers trailing down her neck and then ripping her shirt off. Nausea rose in her throat.

She set her bagel down and mumbled, "Excuse me. I'm not feeling very well." She pushed away from the table and Beckham hurried around to pull her chair out. He wrapped one hand around her elbow and the warmth of that touch made her already shaky legs turn to pudding. Her eyes were drawn to his.

"Thanks," she murmured before withdrawing from his touch and those eyes and fleeing up the stairs. The sanctuary of her room was the only place she wanted to be right now.

Well, he'd tried. Beck finished his breakfast, savoring the sweet papaya and wondering why *tried* was always such a lame word. Tried meant you'd given it an effort. It just didn't seem like enough in this case. Why was Alyssa so offish with him? For a few seconds he felt like they'd connected. She'd looked into his eyes as he studied the dark depths of hers and he'd felt an electricity in the air between them. He'd started imagining all kinds of fun excursions with the beautiful Alyssa over the next week, but then a switch had flipped and she was worse than cold. It was as if he made her physically ill.

He was surprised that he'd been so bold with a stranger. He'd felt an instant connection to her when he'd plowed into her this morning, even though he didn't know anything about her. She was definitely an uncommon beauty with her long, dark hair and that creamy skin, but he'd had a lot of beautiful and successful women hit on him and never felt the way he had the past few minutes around Alyssa. As if they had something between them, some kind of pull.

Maybe it was because she *didn't* seem interested in him. That didn't happen often and it definitely made her more intriguing. It could also be that she had looked as beautiful out running as she did at breakfast. She obviously wasn't a fake, cover herself with a foot of makeup, kind of girl. Her dark eyes lured him in like some kind of siren. That must be it. She was a sea temptress. He laughed to himself and pushed away from the table. A temptress wouldn't turn a guy down stone cold like that.

Beck wondered what he was going to do with himself today. Sitting on a beach always sounded good, but he would probably only last twenty minutes before he'd want to do something active. He decided to just walk around the neighborhood and down to Lahaina. If he couldn't talk a beautiful woman into being his tour guide, he could at least try to enjoy the sites by himself.

By lunchtime Alyssa had several new photographs ready to send to the printers. She used to develop her own originals but found an effective company who did better quality work. They also framed and stored them for her until she was ready to ship to customers or galleries. It saved her a ton of mess and time. Taking pictures was much more fulfilling for her than developing them. She stretched and grabbed her purse. Sunrise Café sounded perfect for lunch.

Walking out of the bed and breakfast and down the street toward Lahaina, she heard a ruckus at the redbrick church on the corner. She glanced over, expecting to see the local boys on their skateboards. When she saw Beckham laughing with some tween boys as they coached him on how to ride one of those crazy Ripstiks, she wished she'd brought her camera along.

She stopped and watched, hoping none of them would look over. Beckham was an art form with his t-shirt clinging to his body as he swiveled his hips to keep the board in motion. The definition in his chest, shoulders, and arms was impressive. Alyssa told herself she was just appreciating the human body like any photographer would do, but this seemed a bit more personal. She was gawking at him because he was not only all man, he had a huge smile and was obviously interacting with these boys on their level.

Beckham ran into the curb and jumped clear of the Ripstik. He threw back his head and laughed and all the boys joined in, chortling and making fun of his crash. Beckham turned and focused right on Alyssa.

She gasped and took a step back. He raised a hand and offered her a friendly smile. She smiled back and waved quickly before striding off down the street. First, she turned him down because she couldn't handle the thought of being alone with a strange man and now she gaped openly at him like a teenage stalker. Her neck was burning hot as she snuck one more glance and found that he was still watching her.

Chapter Four

The next morning, Alyssa gave herself the day off from running and walked to Maulaka Beach so she could photograph the ocean, trees, and turtles. It was pure enjoyment to click some outdoor pictures in the pre-morning light. The pictures she sold were always of people, but it was fun to experiment with landscapes and animals sometimes. How she wished she could've captured those boys and Beckham yesterday. That kind of human interaction was exactly what she thrived on, not to mention she'd love to have a picture of Beckham for herself. She didn't know if she would've dared sell them though. As a photographer she could photograph anyone and everyone who was in a public place, but she'd already taken pictures of Beckham she wasn't proud of. She didn't want to have any other pictures to make him think she was paparazzi if he ever got to know her and put two and two together.

She came back to the outdoor breakfast early and thought she'd be able to enjoy the spread alone, but Beckham was already seated at one of the tables. She was tempted to smile and rush past, maybe come back to eat later, but when he glanced up and grinned at her it was like a cord drew her right in. She nodded to him and went to fill her plate with fruit, granola, and yogurt.

Encouraged by his warm look and the hope that he really wasn't like the wealthy men her dad pushed on her, she walked straight to his table and asked, "Is this seat taken?"

"All the other tables are full?" Beck's wide grin tempered the teasing.

Alyssa laughed. "Guess I deserved that."

Beck stood and took her plate from her hands, brushing her fingers in the process. Tingles shot through Alyssa. She swallowed and could hardly think straight. He set the plate down and then pulled out her chair. "Please, sit with me."

Alyssa felt a jolt of nerves as a flashback came. She couldn't even remember the man's name or what he looked like except for greased black hair, but she could smell his spicy cologne and the way he'd asked her to please, sit with me, before he pulled her onto his lap. She'd been sixteen and it was one of her dad's dinner parties. Taking a long breath, she reminded herself they were in a semi-public place and Beckham seemed like a really nice guy. He wasn't going to make any untoward advances when one of the other guests or Jerry could come to breakfast any time.

"Thanks," she murmured.

She sat and started eating her yogurt slowly, wondering how to start up a conversation. "Did you have a nice first day on the island?" she finally asked.

Beckham's face lit up. "It was great. Some boys taught me to Ripstik."

Alyssa blushed, knowing he'd seen her there.

"Then I found a great place to surf on the northwest end."

"Sounds... great." She almost rolled her eyes when she imitated the adjective he'd already used twice.

"Do you like to surf?" he asked.

Alyssa wondered how to answer that. She would love to try to surf, but with her foot her balance was too far off. "Um, I bodysurf or boogie board."

"Maybe I could teach you."

His blue eyes were so full of hope. She'd shot him down yesterday to tour the island together, and although she wasn't ready to break her rule about being alone with a man she didn't know, she hated to tell him no again. Maryn would probably tell her to break the rule she'd made after her dad forced her into a car alone with one of his politician friends. She'd been seventeen and terrified as the man clasped his long fingers around her thigh. Luckily, she'd been able to get out at a stop light and run until Maryn found her.

"Ally-girl. Hello!"

Alyssa's head jerked up. That voice could only be one person. Granny Ellie rounded the corner of the building on Jerry's arm. Jerry pulled several designer pieces of luggage. They both grinned as they saw Alyssa and Beckham seated together. Alyssa jumped to her feet and ran the few steps to wrap her tiny grandmother in her arms. Worry swept over Alyssa. Was Granny too thin? Her grandmother had fought and won against breast cancer eight years ago, but Alyssa always worried that it would come back. Plus, Granny was getting up in years, any number of things could rob Alyssa of the only family member who loved her unconditionally. Hugging her grandmother, she was safe. The feeling of coming home was overshadowed by knowing Beckham watched and would soon meet her grandmother, who'd never tried to install a filter between her thoughts and her words.

Jerry swept past them. "I'll just take your luggage upstairs."

"Thanks, Jerry, you're a gem."

"Granny?" Alyssa finally managed. "What are you doing here?"

"Idaho's too cold this time of year. Your emails made me worry about my lonely little girl, so I caught a plane." She tapped Alyssa's cheek with her palm. "You look gorgeous, love, but are you so tired of being alone?"

Alyssa glanced to Beckham. He met her gaze then took a drink of his juice.

"Just lonely for you," Alyssa said.

"Ha! I know you're too busy for this old lady. Don't worry, Jerry has a room for me, I'll enjoy the island and you can fit me in during your spare time." She walked purposefully toward Beckham, tugging Alyssa along. "*Who* is this?"

Beckham stood and extended his hand, completely engulfing Granny's fingers with his own. Two feet taller and with all those nicely-formed muscles, the contrast between Beckham and her petite grandmother would make an unreal photograph.

"I'm Beck," he offered.

Granny held onto his hand and tilted her head to the side. "Alyssa's friend? Boyfriend? Fiancé?" She paused and winked. "Make-out buddy?"

"Granny! We haven't even really met." How embarrassing. Granny would have to throw in the make-out buddy. Did she even know what that meant?

"Not officially anyway," Beck said with a smile.

"Oh, so you're free? You ever heard of a cougar?" Granny Ellie made a sound that was somewhere between a meow and a growl and batted her fake eyelashes at him.

"Granny!" Alyssa wanted to go bury herself in the sand.

Beck laughed. "It's nice to meet you, Mrs…"

"Ms. Armsworth. Recently widowed. You can call me Ellie."

"Oh, I'm sorry to hear about your husband, Ellie."

She waved a hand. "It's all right. I liked him, but once you bury four you start getting a little calloused. That's why I'm looking for a younger man." She winked obnoxiously.

Alyssa narrowed her eyes. She knew Granny had loved and mourned each of her husbands. What was she playing at?

"And this is my gorgeous, talented, and oh so sweet, granddaughter, Alyssa."

Alyssa scowled at her.

"What?" Granny raised her shoulders. "You said you hadn't met. Now use those manners I taught you."

Alyssa rolled her eyes and extended her hand. "Alyssa Armsworth. It's nice to meet you."

Beck took her hand between both of his and looked deeply into her eyes. "The pleasure is mine."

Oh, my. She felt like she was a princess and he was the knight coming to formerly court her. Granny cackled and rubbed her small hands together. "This is going to be fun." She linked an arm through Alyssa's elbow and held her other hand out to Beck. "So, kids, how are you going to entertain an old lady today?"

"Granny!" Alyssa shook her head and met Beck's amused glance. "I'm sorry," she told him. "I'm sure you have plans."

"I promised myself I'd try to sit on the beach, but it would be much more fun with you two."

"Oh, yes it would." Granny cocked her head to the side and gave his hand a squeeze. "I tell you what. Let's go down to Ka'anapali Beach and rent us some nice lounge chairs and shade. We'll watch the whales and the waves, I'll take a nap to get over this jet lag, and you and Alyssa can get to know each other better."

"Great idea." Beck's smile swung from Granny to Alyssa. "Let me go put on a swimsuit."

"We'll meet you back here in a few minutes." Granny said. She waited until he walked away and then grinned at Alyssa. "Seeing that man in a swimsuit will be worth the six hour redeye."

"Granny," Alyssa protested half-heartedly. She couldn't hold in a laugh, agreeing with Granny's desire to see Beckham in a suit. A picture formed in her mind and she started to salivate. Too bad she didn't dare bring her camera.

Chapter Five

Beck ran up the stairs to his room. His stomach bubbled with nervous anticipation. He couldn't remember the last time he'd been this excited. Alyssa was beautiful and intriguing and her grandmother was hilarious.

He *had* promised himself he'd sit on the beach, so he hadn't lied to Ellie. Going to the beach with Alyssa and her feisty grandmother was perfect. Tomorrow he planned to meet with some youth coordinators for a troubled teen program in the morning then finally locate the photographer, A.A. Beck had been able to trace the photographer to Maui and found a gallery showing he was going to appear at. Beck wanted to convince the guy to join forces with him and hopefully get him to leave the privileged shores of Maui and go to some developing nations to photograph and help spread the word about children in need. Beck needed this break from his usual reality and finding A.A. would be a huge boost to his efforts. Meeting someone like Alyssa was a bonus he never planned on.

He changed into his swimsuit and pulled a T-shirt over his scarred torso. How would Alyssa react when she saw how abused his body looked? The standard cover story would have to work—too many hits from hockey. He wondered if he'd ever reveal the true story to Alyssa, but quickly forced the idea from his brain. He hardly knew her.

Beck offered to drive and Alyssa barely hid her surprise that his rental car was a Hyundai Elantra. It was hard to believe that a guy this genuine could be a multi-millionaire, or as some sources claimed, a billionaire. Maybe Maryn was right and Beck was kind and down-to-earth. Alyssa almost wasn't afraid for him to see her foot or to be alone with him. They parked at the Marriott and if he noticed her limping toward the beach he didn't say anything. He escorted Granny Ellie on his arm and it was so cute to see the tiny woman beaming up at him and saying all manner of things to embarrass and endear herself to him as only her Granny could do. Beck rented three chaise lounges and two umbrellas. They sat down and Alyssa debated when to take her tennis shoes off. It probably looked awkward with her swimsuit and sarong, but she wasn't ready to see the look of disgust, compassion, or whatever would be on Beck's face when he caught a glimpse of her foot.

After less than a minute, Granny Ellie announced, "Well, this relaxing has been delightful, but it's time for me to shop."

Alyssa and Beck both stood.

"Where are we going shopping?" Alyssa asked, wishing she could sit back down and get to know Beck a little better.

"Not *we*, me." Granny jabbed a finger at herself, eyes twinkling. "You two adorable people are going to cozy up and get to know each other. I'm going to walk to Whaler's Square and spend some of my money and scope out the men. There are bound to be some handsome Tongans in Hawaii." She winked.

Oh, Granny. The woman was addicted to checking out men, especially Tongan men who reminded her of her second husband, Hubba Bubba. Beck chuckled and Alyssa loved the deep, mellow sound of it. It was such a relief he seemed to be enjoying her grandmother. Some people got offended by Granny, but Alyssa just loved her.

"I hate to have you go alone," Alyssa protested feebly. She did want to be with Granny, but Beck was so intriguing. They were in a very public place so she could get to know him without breaking her rule of not being alone with a man she didn't know. It was perfect, but should she really let Granny go alone? They hadn't even had a chance to talk and Alyssa didn't know how Granny's health was faring.

Granny waved her off. "I'll bring back ice cream. What's your flavor?" she asked Beck.

"Anything that has fruit or nuts."

"Did he just say I'm fruity and nuts?" Ellie winked at Alyssa.

Beck laughed and leaned back against the cushioned chair.

"I know your flavor," Granny said to Alyssa, "Chocolate, chocolate, and more chocolate."

"Some things never change." It meant so much that Granny did know. If someone asked one of Alyssa's parents they'd probably be shocked she dared eat fattening ice cream. Her mom worked most of her life to keep her girlish figure and try to keep her dad interested and her dad only thought of women as objects who had to look perfect to be worthwhile.

Granny waved and toddled off. Alyssa was saddened to notice how slow she moved. Maybe she was just worn out from the plane ride. Granny had been such a wonderful part of Alyssa's life, she hoped she'd have years before Granny passed away and left her behind.

"Ellie's great," Beck said.

"She's been there for me through a lot." Alyssa realized she didn't want to explain that one if he asked so she hurried on, "She always makes me laugh. Sorry about the cougar comment."

"I didn't know whether to laugh or run." He winked.

Alyssa's throat went dry. Did she tell him thank you for not running and beg him to never run from them? Wow. She was getting more than a little ahead of herself, but that wink and the sensual look in those blue eyes had her head spinning.

They sat in silence for a few minutes, listening to the waves break and watching two little boys pack sand into a lopsided castle. Several groups of whales spouted off the nearby coastline of Lanai then dove and waved goodbye with their tails.

"What was Ellie saying about how talented you are?" Beck asked.

"Granny likes to brag about me. I'm not that talented. Do you want to walk down and test the water?"

"Um, sure." His face filled with confusion, but he didn't question her further. She really didn't want to tell him she was a photographer, not yet.

They both stood. She untied her sarong and sat it on the chair while he slipped off his flip-flops. She looked at his t-shirt and caught him glancing at her shoes at the same time.

"Do you want to get your shoes wet?"

She took a deep breath. "Do you want your t-shirt soggy?"

He inhaled sharply then smiled. His ruggedly handsome face made her lean against the lounge for support.

"I'll take off my t-shirt if you take off your shoes."

She studied him for a second, sensing he was as uncomfortable taking off his t-shirt as she was removing her shoes and socks. Finally, she nodded. "On the count of three."

His smile grew. "One, two, three."

She bent down and unlaced her shoes while he tugged his shirt over his head and dropped it on his chair. She paused to look up, gasping at the breadth and sculpture of his chest, shoulders, and arms. "Did hockey do that to you?"

Oh, crap! He'd never told her he played hockey. She needed to remember what info he'd actually told her and what she knew from Maryn's files.

He pointed to several vicious scars on his chest and abdomen. "Yep."

"Oh, I didn't mean those, I meant the, um, muscles." She blushed in embarrassment and returned to removing her shoes, grateful he hadn't called her on the slip.

His deep chuckle brought her head up. "Thanks for noticing the muscle before the scars."

"Any woman would." She immediately reddened and focused on pulling off her socks. Standing, she walked toward the water, her limp much more pronounced without her inserts. She jabbed her foot into the squishy sand with each step, the granules almost covered her partially-formed right foot.

Beck quickly reached her side and held onto her elbow, steadying her. She glanced up at him, appreciating his warm touch. "Thank you."

"Sure. Do you mind me asking what happened?"

"Birth defect." Had any man ever cared about what happened to her foot? Most had ignored it or tried to ignore it. Her dad had paid for numerous surgeries to fix the defect but when you were born without your fourth and fifth toe and a third of your foot, it was pretty hard to implant that.

"Thank you for taking your shoes off," he whispered next to her ear.

Alyssa turned, his face was close as he bent toward her, and she focused on how well-formed his lips were, shapely and intriguing. She trailed her gaze from his face down to his muscular shoulders and blushed again. "Thank you for taking your shirt off."

He chuckled and they walked straight into the water. It was a little cool, but still felt wonderful with the warm sun overhead. Alyssa couldn't believe how understanding and gracious Beck had been about her foot. He hadn't seemed embarrassed for her or embarrassed to be with her.

"Are we swimming or just wading?" Beck asked.

"Oh, we're swimming." Alyssa pressed on until the water was waist-deep then broke from his grip and performed a shallow dive.

Beck appeared by her side, swimming through the waves. "I knew I liked you, Alyssa Armsworth."

"What did I do that made you like me?" She smiled at him, treading water and looking into his blue eyes that gave the water competition for sparkle.

"You're not a sit around and suntan kind of girl. You're a get in the water and enjoy it kind."

"Life's too short for skin cancer," she said.

He laughed.

A large wave came toward them and Alyssa started swimming freestyle to catch it. The wave slid up and over her and then she was in the middle of it and it pushed her forward in its trough. She came up out of it, sputtering water and grinning from the rush. Beck stood a few feet away, a similar smile on his face. He gestured with his head and they both swam back out to catch the next one.

After several successful rides, they treaded water side by side, basically floating in the salt water. Alyssa couldn't believe how relaxing it was to be with this man compared to the many horrifying experiences she'd had with other men. She didn't want to be some man hater, but she usually found it easier just to avoid the opposite sex.

"So how does body surfing compare to real surfing?" she asked.

Beck met her gaze and the compassion she hated to see was there. "I'm sorry. When I asked you if you wanted to learn to surf this morning I didn't know..."

Alyssa nodded. "It's okay. It's no big deal. I just can't balance as well as I'd like sometimes."

"I'm sorry you can't surf, but this is almost as much fun." The sun glinted off his wet, dark hair and his broad shoulders.

"Almost?" Alyssa smiled to let him know she was teasing.

"Well, you wouldn't want me to lie to you, would you?" Beck grinned.

Alyssa's breath caught in her throat. She stopped treading water and swallowed a bit of sea water. She spit it out. "Excuse me. No, I definitely wouldn't want you to lie to me."

The moment turned serious as she studied Beck and he returned her gaze with those clear, blue eyes. Was he really as genuine as he appeared or would he turn into an obnoxious octopus given the opportunity? Alyssa heard a wave coming and took the chance to end the staring contest, swimming quickly into the froth. It collapsed earlier than she thought and she was rolled along the ocean floor, salt water filling her mouth and nose. She came up spitting and coughing. Beck was immediately by her side.

"You all right?"

"Granny always told me not to drink the ocean."

Beck laughed, but still looked concerned.

Alyssa pushed against his shoulder, loving the feel of those smooth, rounded muscles. "Of course I'm all right. Race you out there." She dove into the water and swam for the deeper part of the ocean. Beck was unreal. He appeared to sincerely care, he was fun to be with, and he was very easy on the eyes. She needed to be very, very careful. The different men who'd tried to claim her over the years had taught her to be vigilant, especially when someone seemed too good to be true.

They body surfed the rolling waves for a while until Granny Ellie called from the beach, waving cups of ice cream. Swimming side by side, Alyssa glanced over at Beck. She loved the way he looked with his strong body and handsome face, but she liked the way he treated her and Granny even more. She stood in the shallow waves and he immediately offered his elbow. Alyssa leaned against him as they slogged their way through the sand to Granny Ellie.

"I wasn't sure how to keep it cold while I walked back, so you have melted cream instead of ice cream," Granny handed them each a cup after they toweled off.

"Still tastes good," Beck said, drinking his cup of strawberry cheesecake.

"Your cheek seems to like it too." Alyssa laughed.

Beck looked confused. She reached over and wiped the pink smear from his cheek. Beck captured her hand with his palm and licked the melted ice cream off of her finger. Alyssa almost melted herself until he turned and spit.

"Salt," he managed, grabbing a water bottle from the cooler and taking a long drink.

Alyssa and Granny Ellie laughed.

"Now that was romantic," Granny said.

Beck blushed and drank more water. Alyssa scooped the chocolate chunks up and savored the richness of dark chocolate. Granny had been joking about it being romantic, but the warmth of his tongue on her finger had done crazy things to her insides.

"I want to be buried in the sand." Granny stood and walked away from their chairs until she found a nice open spot.

Beck leaned close to Alyssa. "She's joking, right?"

"Who knows? Hopefully she means just for fun and not her actual burial site."

Beck had just taken another drink, but started laughing at her comment. The laugh turned to a cough as he inhaled the water. Alyssa lifted his left arm. "Take a deep breath," she instructed.

His coughing calmed but they stayed in the awkward position of her holding his much thicker arm aloft and staring at each other. Alyssa was having crazy thoughts like wanting to run her fingers down his arm and maybe tickle the side of his chest.

"I'm ready for my burial," Granny Ellie called from the beach.

Alyssa dropped Beck's arm and stood.

Beck strode to Granny's side. "We have to do this right." He used his forearm to scoop out sand until there was a nice depression, then formed a sort of pillow on the end. "Lay in that."

Granny Ellie obeyed. Alyssa and Beck started scooping sand over her small frame.

"I never knew this was how you wanted to be laid to rest," Alyssa said, trying not to laugh at the image they were making. Two adults covering a tiny elderly woman in sand like they were all a bunch of children.

"Just burn me when I croak," Ellie said, closing her eyes and seeming to enjoy the sand covering her. "And only a quick service. I hate the blubbering at funerals. Oh, and lots of yummy food. Feed everybody."

"I was joking." Alyssa's joy evaporated as she imagined really burying her beloved grandmother. She'd be so alone, but Granny wasn't going anywhere for a long, long time. At least Alyssa hoped not. She looked up to see Beck studying her. She forced a smile and scooped more sand to cover Granny's legs.

They kept piling sand on until Granny whispered, "Okay. I think that's good."

Alyssa met Beck's eye and the laughter just spilled out. They laughed so hard her stomach hurt.

"Get a picture quick and get me out of here," Granny demanded.

Beck and Alyssa handed their phones to a teenage boy tossing a football nearby. Alyssa wished she had her high quality camera. She wanted to remember this moment forever and she'd really like to zoom in on Beck's chest.

The young man took the first picture with each of them on one side before Granny demanded, "No. You both need to be on my right so the sun won't ruin the picture."

Alyssa laughed at Granny telling her how to pose for a picture, but she obediently moved next to Beck and knelt in the squishy sand.

"Put your arm around her, act like you actually like us," Granny told Beck.

He shrugged and smiled at Alyssa. "Does anyone ever tell her no?"

"Why would anyone want to?" Granny squeaked. "Hurry up, I'm being crushed by sand granules here!"

Beck wrapped his arm around Alyssa and drew her into his side. Alyssa should've stayed more upright but she found herself leaning against him and wrapping her arms around his chiseled abdomen. Her fingers touched the bumpy scars there and he stiffened for a second before relaxing and bringing his other hand to her waist. Tingles shot through her body from his firm hand.

It felt so natural to be cuddled up like this, but at the same time more exciting than skydiving. Alyssa's pulse was thundering in her throat and she couldn't create any moisture in her mouth. She'd dated different men since being attacked by Hugh and though a lot of them had been nice guys she'd always felt tense and afraid when they touched her. Right now the only emotions were excitement and warmth. Was it Beck or was she finally ready to be close to a man again?

Alyssa smiled for the shots, sad when the boy declared he had some good ones and extended their phones in his hand. Was it her imagination or did Beck let go almost as slowly as she did?

Beck stood and retrieved their phones while Alyssa started

pushing the sand off of her grandmother. Granny looked at her and winked. "Now that was more like it."

Beck joined them and Alyssa was relieved she didn't have to tell Granny to knock it off because really, she didn't want her to. Usually when Granny tried to push her toward men she balked and ran the other direction. With Beck, she wanted to run right to him.

Alyssa enjoyed every minute with Beck. She thought of how Maryn had asked her to secure a date with him and hoped this counted, but she also hoped this was just the beginning. Then realization poured over her. She couldn't become involved with him. If she did, she'd have to confess to taking pictures of him and his sister and selling them to a magazine that distorted the truth and sold millions of copies of that distortion. Then she would see hurt and anger instead of laugher and appreciation in his eyes. That could never happen.

Chapter Six

"No way!" Maryn screamed into the phone. "You spent the day with him? On the beach?"

"He's... impressive." Alyssa wasn't sure that was the right description of Beck. He was handsome, fun, smart, kind, and she was definitely impressed. She unwound the towel from her head, playing in the ocean and sand had been great but her hair needed that scrubbing.

"Details!"

"There's not much to tell. We met this morning at breakfast. Granny asked him to go to the beach with us and we had a great time. Swimming, snorkeling, burying Granny in the sand, lunch at Hulu Grill."

"Granny Ellie is such a hoot."

"Yes, she is."

"And... how does he look without his shirt on?"

Alyssa drew in a sharp breath and placed her hand on her heart. "Fabulous."

"I knew it! I knew it! Can you send me a pic?"

"If you promise not to use it for some stupid article." Alyssa hated that she worried. Maryn was her best friend, but she was also a voracious magazine writer and Beckham Taylor was prime writing material.

"I promise. Sheesh. What do you take me for?"

"I feel awful about taking those pics of him, Mar." She ran a brush through her hair, tugging at a knot.

"I know, but he'll probably never know it was you."

Him not discovering the truth didn't make Alyssa feel much better.

A pounding at the door announced Granny Ellie, dressed in a silky pant suit, looking classy and beautiful. "Hang up the phone and get ready," she instructed. "Beck is taking us to Kimo's."

"I gotta go," Alyssa told Maryn. "I'll send a pic soon." She hung up amidst much protest. "You talked him into taking us to dinner too?"

"Didn't take much talking." Granny winked. "What have you got to wear?" She started yanking dresses out of Alyssa's closet.

"Wait. I don't want you pushing him into dating me."

"Who's granddaughter are you?" She held up a knee-length floral dress and tossed it at Alyssa. "A fine-looking, intelligent, fun-loving, and possibly wealthy—I'm still doing a little sleuthing to determine that one—man is interested. And wow if he isn't a lot of man. You push, drag, beat him over the head if you have to, but you do not play hard to get. Got it?"

Alyssa barely hid the rolling of her eyes. At least Granny hadn't called Maryn yet and found out the whole scoop. She darted to the bathroom to change, put on some minimal makeup, and see what she could do with her hair. "Give me ten minutes."

"I'll see you in the courtyard in five." Granny Ellie slammed the door on the way out.

Alyssa laughed as she slipped on her dress. "'Who's granddaughter are you?'" Then she sobered as she looked in the mirror at her dark skin and hair. She loved being Granny Ellie's, but sadly she was a product of her mother too and her mother had taught her that men, especially wealthy ones, only make you miserable.

Beck paced the courtyard waiting for Alyssa to appear.

"Calm it," Ellie commanded. "She'd be an imbecile to not want a taste of you tonight. Raar." She batted her eyelashes and smiled coyly at him.

"Ellie." Beck stopped walking and shook his head at the older woman. "I barely know her and she's your granddaughter. Shouldn't you be protecting her from me?"

Ellie met his gaze, her blue eyes full of mischief. "You know everybody has talents?"

"Sure."

"I have a talent that I've honed to perfection throughout the years—knowing if a man is worth his weight in gold… or not. Four different husbands and they were all worth it, even though it about killed me to lose them." She glanced up and down his frame. "You're a big one, but I still think I'm dead on that you're worth every pound."

Beck chuckled, wondering for a second if Granny knew how wealthy he was. He weighed over two hundred and fifty pounds and when he first took over his family's business it had been worth two hundred and fifty million dollars. The analogy would have worked then though he'd grown his net worth considerably in the past couple of years buying and building a considerable amount of commercial real estate in Orange County. "Thanks, I think."

He heard a light tread and turned to see Alyssa descending the stairs in a flowing dress, the bright colors accentuating the beauty of her dark coloring. Her shapely calf muscles were on fine display, but he noticed she wore a sturdy, but feminine shoes instead of a sandal like most women would. He loved that she'd entrusted him with her birth defect. He loved each minute he'd spent with her today. Thanks to her hilarious grandmother their time was going to be extended.

He didn't appreciate shallow women, the kind that came onto him easily because of his fame and money. A lot of those women appeared, on the outside to have it all together, but once he dug to the inside there was nothing there, exactly like his ex-girlfriend Belle. From all he'd seen, Alyssa was very different from the women who pursued him. He liked that although it obviously hurt her to run she didn't slow down or stop but kept working hard. He liked that her life didn't appear to be easy, but she had fun and was sweet with her grandmother and everyone else he'd seen her interact with, from the teenage boys gawking at her on the beach to the old men gawking at her at the restaurant. He could tell she was a good person—being beautiful was actually just a bonus. A nice bonus.

"Alyssa." His voice came out all breathy and embarrassing. He cleared his throat. "You look amazing."

"Thanks." She met his gaze and smiled. "You're looking pretty good yourself."

"Slight improvement from being covered in salt and sand."

"Ha!" Granny Ellie clasped her hands together, grinning at the two of them. "I was the one plastered in sand. Well, you two have fun. I'm heading to bed." She took a step toward the stairs.

"Oh, no, you don't." Alyssa grabbed her grandmother's arm. "Beck asked you to dinner, not me."

Beck laughed. "I don't want to steal your granddaughter on your first night on the island."

"Oh, pooh," Ellie said. "Don't you think you deserve something special tonight, not a dinner with an old geezer?"

"It will be special going to dinner with two beautiful ladies."

Ellie shook her head, but wrapped her hand through the elbow he offered. Alyssa placed her warm hand on his other elbow and Beck straightened. He felt like the king of the world with her close to him.

41

Alyssa was grateful Granny hadn't dodged out of their dinner date. She was interested in Beck, but she still wasn't ready to be alone with any man.

She hadn't eaten at Kimo's before. They had a beautiful view of the setting sun from the second story balcony. The restaurant didn't appear too extravagant—scarred, wood tables and floors. The only thing pompous was their starched shirt waiter and the fancy menu.

Jerry from the bed and breakfast had advised her when she first arrived on the island, "If you're willing to take out a second mortgage, eat at Kimo's or Mama's Fish House." As Alyssa didn't have a first mortgage she'd steered clear, but all the food on the island was expensive so she wasn't shocked when most of the entrees were fifty dollars or more.

"Holy stink," Granny Ellie exclaimed. "Did they import the fish from Alaska? Look at these prices."

Beck smiled, not seeming the least bit embarrassed. The waiter shifted from foot to foot. "I assure you ma'am, the fish is local and fresh and it is worth every penny."

"Is that so?" Granny glanced up at him. "You pay full price here on a regular basis?"

He cleared his throat. "Um, no, ma'am. Can I start you with something to drink?"

They all ordered water which seemed to supremely disappoint the waiter. He swept the wine menus off the table, made his recommendations for dinner, and then left.

Granny looked at Beck. "I'm sorry I suggested coming here. I asked some locals while I was out shopping and they said it was the best. We can leave or go Dutch, but I am *not* letting you pay for this dinner."

Beck chuckled long and low. "Ellie, it is just fine, I promise."

She leaned back and studied him like she would her poker rivals. "What do you do for work that you can travel to Hawaii, spend the day frolicking in the sun, and say that a dinner like this," she gestured to the menu, "is no worry?"

"Granny," Alyssa reprimanded. He was going to think they were after him for his money. Alyssa sank deeper into her chair. What would he think when he found out she had photographed him for Maryn's scummy magazines? Forget that Beck was handsome and fabulous, this was a very bad idea.

"It's okay." Beck reassured Alyssa with a smile and a nod. He tilted his head to the side and focused on Granny. "I manage real estate and charitable foundations."

Granny pursed her lips. "So you're basically independently wealthy. I *knew* it."

Beck shifted uncomfortably and looked at his menu.

"Do you realize, young man, that you have never told us your full name?"

Beck's gaze lifted again. Alyssa felt bad for him and wished she knew how to call Granny off without embarrassing him more. He obviously didn't want people to know who he was and she'd known all along because of Maryn, and Granny was going to rip it out of him whether he wanted to share or not.

"Why is that?" Granny asked. "You one of those who wants women to like him for who he is before they find out he's wealthy? I can promise you we aren't gold miners."

Alyssa groaned and Beck's true smile came out. "You know what, Ellie? I believe neither of you are after me for my money. My full name is Beckham Taylor."

How did he believe they weren't after him for his money? Alyssa wanted him to keep believing that because she really wasn't, but she knew that wouldn't be the case if he ever connected the dots that she had sold both of their souls years ago for money.

Granny's mouth twisted. "I don't keep up on the celebrity rags. Why are you famous?"

"I'm not famous. I had a decent career in the NHL and now I manage my family's businesses."

"Why didn't you tell us your last name when we first met?"

"Some people recognize it and you're right, I'd rather avoid those who are after me for my family money."

Alyssa felt bad for him. Her dad had money but she'd distanced herself at eighteen and fought through life on her own, no matter how many times her dad tried to reenter her world. With Beck's parents' deaths, that wasn't an option for him. She shuddered at the thought of being involved in her father's businesses. Hopefully there was a world of difference between the underhanded deals her father made and Beck's real estate and charitable foundations. She'd place money on it.

"So you're rich, but you stay at a cheap bed and breakfast and drive a piece of shmack Hyundai to remain humble?"

Beck laughed. "Something like that."

"So you're telling me to order the market fish?"

"Order whatever you like."

The waiter arrived with their waters and Granny did order whatever she liked. Alyssa exchanged a secret smile with Beck. She'd met few men who could deal so well with her Granny. Even though he was affluent, Beck didn't try to flaunt it or control others because of it and from what Maryn had told her, he was managing the family business because of his family's need of his business sense and level head. Once again, she was impressed.

Dinner passed quickly and even Granny had to admit the mahi-mahi was worth the price, which finally brought a discreet smile to their waiter's face.

They stood to walk out and Granny declared, "I love walking by the water at night. Will you two walk with me?"

"Sure," Beck said.

Alyssa wondered what Granny was up to, but she also loved to walk by the water at night and rarely dared to do it alone. She caught Beck's gaze over Granny's head and smiled. "That sounds great."

They walked casually down to the beach, passing a huge Tongan man. Granny batted her eyelashes and called out, "Hello, Handsome."

He grinned back at her. "Hello, Beautiful Lady."

Granny sighed and turned to watch him go. "Makes me miss my Hubba Bubba."

Alyssa smiled. She missed Hubba Bubba too, he was the closest thing to a grandfather she'd ever had and always had a huge smile on his face.

Beck didn't question Granny checking out men half her age and they continued along the sand. The sun had set but a half moon reflected off the water and the light from the restaurants and businesses improved visibility. The mild weather and soothing crash of waves made it a perfect night for a walk.

Granny released Beck's arm and came around to the other side of Alyssa. "I want to be closer to the water," she said. She kept tugging Alyssa until their shoes were getting wet. Suddenly, she screeched and fell toward the water. Alyssa released her grip on Beck and reached for Granny to try to pull her back. Granny shifted her weight and pushed Alyssa. Alyssa stumbled into the water with a gasp.

"Help her," Granny demanded of Beck.

Beck rushed to Alyssa's aid, but must've tripped on something. He sprawled on top of Alyssa and knocked her farther into the sand and the surf. Granny edged up the beach toward the sidewalk.

Beck's weight pressed against Alyssa for half a second and even though he was heavy, she liked being close to him.

He quickly lifted himself off of Alyssa and pulled her to her feet. A wave came in and pushed her off-balance and against his chest. His arms wrapped around her. Alyssa knew it was probably just instinct that made him hug her, but it felt wonderful and she naturally looked up into his blue eyes reflected from the half-moon.

"You okay?" he asked, his voice huskier than usual.

"Wet, but I'll survive."

His deep chuckle reverberated against her chest. She pressed herself closer and darn if those lips weren't tugging at her. His arms and chest felt so strong, so comforting. It was the comfort of home and the overwhelming excitement of an amazing and handsome man being close. Had anyone's touch felt like this? Was it just because it had been so long since she'd allowed a man close?

A wave came again. Alyssa stutter-stepped and came back to her senses. She forced her focus away from his lips and glanced up the beach for Granny.

"Where did she go?"

Granny had disappeared.

"I don't know," Beck said, "but I'm pretty sure she tripped me."

Alyssa stepped out of the circle of his arms, regretting every movement that took her away from him, but grateful that he let her go. That alone told her he was different from the men who'd tried to take advantage of her. She slogged her way up the beach. Beck stayed close with his hand on her elbow. Even that small touch had her quivering.

"I think she pushed me," Alyssa admitted. "Scheming old woman."

"She definitely knows what she wants," Beck said.

Alyssa swallowed, not responding to that comment. Granny obviously wanted to see the two of them together and Maryn's plotting was adding to that. What would Granny do if she knew about

Maryn's scheme? She'd tell Alyssa to be honest, but how could she tell Beck what Maryn had asked her to do? What she'd done for her friend in the past? He obviously liked his privacy and she didn't want to ruin the mood of the night or destroy his entire opinion of her. Even getting one of her favorite dresses wet and sandy was worth the time she'd spent in Beck's arms.

They found Granny waiting by the car. "How was the swim?" she asked, a twinkle in her eyes.

"Refreshing," Alyssa muttered. "Why did you leave?"

"I didn't want to interrupt anything."

Alyssa blushed. She glanced at Beck, who smiled, shook his head, and hurried to open the door for Granny.

"Nothing to interrupt," Alyssa said.

"Dang, girl," Granny shook her head in disappointment. "Have I taught you nothing about capitalizing on opportunities?"

Beck laughed and then coughed. He helped Granny into the car then opened the door for Alyssa.

"I'm sorry," she whispered.

"The only thing you should be sorry about is the missed opportunity." He winked and helped her into the car.

Alyssa tingled from his look and his wink.

Chapter Seven

Alyssa didn't see Beck the next morning at breakfast. It was odd that she missed him. They'd only met two days ago yet she already looked for him and wanted to hear what he would say about Granny's antics or feel the tingly sensation of his touch.

She and Granny spent the morning shopping in the little boutique stores in Lahaina. Granny hit it off with the employees at Maui Built. They looked a little rough around the edges, but Granny had them all laughing and promising to say their prayers before she and Alyssa made their purchases.

After a light lunch at Cool Cat Café, Alyssa changed into a pale blue suit with a short-sleeved jacket and knee-length skirt for her showing that afternoon. She usually loved meeting fans and talking to people about her photography, but knowing that Beck's itinerary said he was planning to come to the gallery had her tied in knots. Maybe Maryn was wrong and he wouldn't really show up. He hadn't stayed at the Marriott like Maryn thought he would so maybe his agenda regarding A.A. had changed also.

Alyssa wanted to see him again, but she didn't want him to think she'd been trying to hide anything, even though she was. Aargh. This was a mess. They'd had a great time yesterday, but really hadn't gotten into careers with the exception of Granny pinning Beck down about what he did. Should she have told him who she was? Should she have spilled the whole story of Maryn knowing so much about him and asking Alyssa to get a date? She didn't want to know if he would be more disappointed or angry when he found out because even though she had a hard time trusting men in general there was something about Beck. He was the stuff of her innocent self's daydreams. Those dreams had been shattered, but there were still pieces of her who wanted a man like Beck to come to her rescue.

She rapped on Granny's door then swung it open to find her lying on the bed. "I'm off to the gallery. Do you want to come?"

"That's a long time to sit and you wore me out shopping. Do you mind if I rest then we'll do something fun tonight?"

"No, that sounds great." Alyssa chewed on her cheek, forgetting her own worries as she stewed over whether Granny was simply tired or if something more serious was going on. Granny had never missed an opportunity to see Alyssa shine before and her showings were few and far between. No, she was overanalyzing. Granny had been to plenty of her art shows and she had every right to be worn out. Older people just tired more easily. Yet there was a frailty to Granny that Alyssa hadn't seen since her bout with cancer years ago. *Please don't let her get cancer again*, Alyssa prayed.

"Have fun, love."

Alyssa blew her a kiss and shut the door, saddened by how fragile and tired she looked. Granny Ellie had always been so vibrant and such a huge part of her life. Since Alyssa had shut herself out of her parents' messed-up relationship years ago, Granny was the only family she had. But love and her granddaughter's fear of loneliness couldn't stop the aging process. It broke Alyssa's heart.

She arrived at the gallery early and enjoyed meeting the owners, a fun Hawaiian couple who introduced themselves as Mama Rue and Pa. They had a huge display of her photography. She traced a finger down the photo of her friend, Nikki. She'd taken some photographs of Nikki and her new husband at the wedding in September. Alyssa was thrilled for her friend's happiness—nobody deserved it more than

Nikki, but sometimes the jealousy clenched her insides. As a teenager she used to dream of a husband and beautiful children of her own. Two days ago she would've thought that was an impossible dream, but Beck was breaking down her barriers.

Pa offered her a chair and a bottle of water. Before long she was on her feet answering questions for fans, who'd come specifically to meet her and rave about how much they loved her work, and tourists, who had no clue who she was or why her photography was so expensive. She explained quite a few times that all of her pieces were originals, and she never made prints which increased value and resale. It wasn't unheard of for her photographs to be resold online for many times their original cost. Also, a good portion of the proceeds were donated to orphanages throughout the world. Some of the tourists got excited about her vision and the beautiful pictures and bought their own autographed one. Her loyal fans bought up numerous photographs. She was grateful the gallery had extras on hand. She didn't put any personal information on her website so her fans were always excited to meet her.

"A.A. is really here," a woman shrieked.

Alyssa smiled and stood to greet her. The woman skirted the table next to Alyssa and pulled her into a bone-crunching hug. Alyssa laughed at her exuberance and started signing the pictures the woman thrust at her. "I've bought almost a dozen. I need more. What do you have available today?"

"There are quite a few left," Alyssa said. She glanced over the photographs the woman had already purchased and said, "You'll love the pictures of the children from Hana."

"Oooh! Perfect." The woman handed off the photography she'd brought from home for Alyssa to sign and started perusing the stock on hand. The door creaked open and Alyssa's head jerked up when a broad-shouldered, dark-haired man walked in. Her breath caught. He turned to face her and she deflated. Not Beck. It was okay. She was okay.

A couple of hours flew by and the worry over Beck coming, and then over him not coming, was always there at the corner of her mind. If he never showed up, she wouldn't have to explain everything, but her chest tightened at the thought of not seeing him. She'd become addicted to his grin pretty quick.

While signing an eight by eight photograph and handing it to the smiling woman, and her not-so-smiling husband, who'd paid over two grand for a relatively small picture, Alyssa heard a familiar voice behind her, "So, the famous A.A. is actually my friend, Alyssa Armsworth."

She spun around and sighed his name, "Beck. You came."

He looked good in a short-sleeved button-down shirt and slacks with his dark hair styled perfectly. Okay, better than good, he was "drool-worthy" as Maryn would say.

He cocked his head to the side and his brow furrowed. "Were you expecting me?"

"Um, no. I just kind of hoped you would." She fiddled with some business cards on the table.

"I had no clue A.A. was you." He folded his arms across his chest and she caught a breath at the solidness of his biceps. "Why didn't you tell me? The 'what do you do for work' question usually comes up before the scheming grandmother pushes me into the ocean with a woman."

His smile told her he was teasing, but she still wasn't feeling very comfortable hiding what she knew about him. She bit at her lip and shrugged. "It's not something I tell many people."

He walked a few steps closer. She could smell his intoxicating woodsy cologne. "I kind of hoped I was a bit closer to you than 'many people'. We swam in the ocean together, twice because of Granny Ellie body checking us in last night."

Alyssa let loose the tension she'd held with a laugh. This was Beck. He was so easygoing, nothing seemed to upset him. She'd tell him about Maryn and the tabloid pictures, when the time was right. "Definitely makes us closer. Sorry. There just wasn't a good time to tell you."

He took her hand. "It's okay. Crazy that the reason I came to Maui was to meet you."

"Really?" Her heartbeat quickened at the look in his eyes. *He came to Maui just for me?* Alyssa all but melted at his feet. Was Beck the dream she'd had all those years ago? Before other men ruined her innocent hopes.

"I can't tell you how happy I am that you're A.A." That warmed her all over until he continued, "I have a business proposition for you."

"Huh?" The dreams fragmented again. He hadn't come to fulfill her destiny, he'd come for a "business proposition". Oh, how she hated those words, her dad's favorite phrase, before he manipulated and used her and everybody else he met.

"Are you almost done here?"

Pa gave them a thumbs up. "She's sold almost everything I have in stock. Take her, buddy."

"Take her?" Alyssa mouthed to Beck.

He laughed and wrapped his fingers around her elbow. "You up for an early dinner?"

"Let me just check in with Granny."

"Great."

She placed the call while still staring at Beck. She'd hated the words "business proposition" because of her dad, but she had also learned to be concerned when she heard them because of her talent. She never knew if someone was interested in her for her or for her artwork. That was probably how Beck felt about his wealth. Hmm.

"Hello," Granny Ellie answered.

"Grans, Beck just came to the gallery and wants to take me to dinner. Do you want us to come get you?"

"Heavens, no. I'm going on a nice walk and then I'll eat my leftovers from lunch and watch a chick flick. You two enjoy yourselves."

Granny hung up before she could respond.

"Granny turned me down flat. Guess it's just us." She shivered at the thought of being alone with him, not only was he strong but she was drawn to him like she'd never been to another man. She could easily let her guard down and he could hurt her physically or emotionally, and as much as she liked him, she might never heal.

It's Beck, she kept repeating. *He'd never hurt me.*

But really, did she know that? Did she really know him? He'd flown all the way to Hawaii to find A.A. Maybe he'd known all along who she was. Maybe he had someone like Maryn on his staff who could dig through people's dirt and find out what they wanted. Maybe he was here to proposition her for more than just business. Oh, my heavens, that was silly. He was exquisitely handsome, wealthy, and great to be around. He didn't need to be stalking women.

Dinner alone with him would be fine. They'd be at a crowded restaurant and then if she didn't feel comfortable with him driving her home, she could walk to the bed and breakfast from there.

"Perfect," he said.

Beck offered her a smile and his arm. They walked out into a windy afternoon, but she hardly noticed her hair knotting as she studied Beck. He was extremely handsome in that pale blue color and the soft material of his shirt did nothing to hide the musculature underneath, but for some horrid reason she kept waiting for him to unzip his perfect costume and allow the creep to crawl out. Why did she have to be so untrusting?

They strolled to the Lahaina Pizza Company. Alyssa watched Beck as he asked for a table for two. Polite, friendly, but never leering or smutty. They climbed the stairs to the upper dining area. Her right foot landed halfway onto a step and she flung out her hands to catch herself. Beck steadied her with his firm hands and his warmth lingered even after he pulled her chair out and was no longer touching her. Why couldn't she have some faith that the good Lord hadn't created an entire gender of monsters? She knew that most men were good guys and didn't have hidden agendas, but it was kind of like convincing a two-year old that the dark wasn't scary. She had just been exposed to an excessive amount of greed and lust.

The waitress arrived and Beck looked to Alyssa. "You're the expert here. What should we order?"

"Shrimp thermadour," Alyssa responded without hesitation. Man, he just did everything right, but the words "business proposition" kept repeating in her head.

"Shrimp thermadour," Beck repeated to the waitress, "And two salads?" He smiled at Alyssa.

"Yes, please. Ranch with mine."

"I'll have the house. Thank you." Beck handed the waitress the menus and then fully focused on Alyssa.

She smiled shyly and ducked her head. A few seconds ticked by as Alyssa played with the straw in her water, tucked some hair behind her ear, and finally got brave enough to ask, "Business proposition?"

"You seem... nervous," Beck said.

Alyssa inhaled and then released it. "Sorry. I've had my share of... propositions over the years."

"I bet." His understanding gaze met hers. "So have I."

Something passed between them that was so real she felt she could reach out and hold it. Why couldn't she let go of the distrust and give Beck a chance? A chance at a business proposition or something else? She wasn't sure she was ready to know.

The waitress brought their salads and garlic bread. Alyssa drizzled her greens with ranch and took a bite of the fresh lettuce, mozzarella, and tomatoes. Her stomach tumbled a little bit with the anxiety over what Beck was going to say. She set her fork down and faced him.

"Let's use a different word. Partnership?" Beck leaned forward, his face lit with excitement. "I love your work. I've been following your photography for the past couple years and have bought several pieces for my home and office."

"Thank you." She blushed with the compliment.

"My business takes me all over the world, mostly developing nations who have a lot of need. We do everything from securing clean drinking water to building schools and teaching people how to plant gardens. I'd love for you to come with me. To take pictures of the children—their beauty and their suffering. You have power in your photography that no one else has. I need you, Alyssa."

Beck focused on her and for a moment she forgot her fears and the crowded restaurant around them. She was amazed at how long she could hold his gaze and instead of feeling awkward, wanted to just keep staring into his eyes and communicating without words.

"You need *me?*" her voice cracked and she took a drink of her water to break the intensity of the moment.

"Yes." He placed his hand over hers. Alyssa liked the feel of his large palm on her fingers. "And the children need you. The attention you'll bring to Jordan's Buds could finance clothing, food, water, and so much more. I wish I could self-fund the entire program, but unfortunately a lot of my resources are tied up in real estate, the stock market, and other investments. I only have so much liquid cash to give to the children and the operating costs of Jordan's Buds each month." He glanced down at the table as if embarrassed to be sharing too much.

Alyssa could tell he wasn't bragging about all the money he had, but he really was putting as much as possible into helping others. Driving a cheap rental car and staying in an affordable bed and breakfast proved his point without him having to say anything.

"So you flew to Hawaii, hoping to get A.A. to come with you on trips around the world. What if I was ugly?" Her hands trembled and she had to clench them in her lap.

He barked a short laugh then pressed his lips together and took a drink of his water. "Do you want to know the truth?"

Alyssa braced her hands on the table. Here it was. The truth. She'd been waiting for it to come out, but now she wasn't so sure she wanted to hear it. "Yes," she whispered.

"I thought you were a man."

"What?" Alyssa didn't know whether to laugh or be offended. She looked down at her body. She'd never been mistaken for a man before.

"No!" Beck shook his head, hiding a smile. "Not when I met you. Before I came."

"Why?"

"I'd convinced myself A.A. was a man because a woman would maybe do a first name or not be such an impressive business person." He held up his hands in defense, his face red. "Sorry."

"Chauvinist," she muttered, but she found herself smiling at his honesty and embarrassment.

He chuckled. "I didn't really think too much about what A.A. would be like. I always meant it to be a business deal. I wasn't concerned with anything but A.A.'s photography talent so I didn't concentrate on who he or she was. I have to admit though, knowing you, the idea of traveling together has a lot more appeal."

Alyssa's lips twitched with a smile. She picked up her fork and stabbed some more lettuce before asking, "So you want to hire me, join forces...what?" Was she really considering this? Granny and

Maryn would scream to go for it, but something held her back. She could barely handle going to dinner alone with a man, how in the world was she going to travel with Beck? Would he expect more? Would he pressure her into sharing a room? She shuddered, remembering her college boyfriend, Tyler, and the trip he took her on to Mazatlan. She'd barely noticed the adjoining doors, until he was pawing her in the middle of the night and she had to fight him off.

"Hire you. I wouldn't expect you to donate your time without compensation." He tore off a hunk of garlic bread and slowly chewed. "This is really good."

Alyssa tried a bite, loving the warmth and freshness of the crusty bread. Her stomach was finally settling. "It is. You said you've been following my career..." Alyssa trailed off as an awful thought entered her mind. If he followed her career, did he already know about the pictures she'd taken of him and his sister? She swallowed and continued. "You probably noticed I donate a lot of money to children's charities. Admit it, part of you was hoping I would offer to come for free."

Beck pushed his hand against the lacquered wood table. "With the impact you can make, I'm not worried about the expense of hiring you. Is twenty-thousand a month reasonable? You could have rights to at least half of the pictures you take, and I'll cover all traveling expenses."

Alyssa placed her hand over his. This discussion needed to slow down. She wasn't ready to talk numbers when she still couldn't commit to what he was asking. "Can I have some time to think about it?"

"I'll give you a week, but on one condition. Let me spend the week with you and convince you I'll be the best work buddy you'll ever have." He held her gaze, not winking or pumping eyebrows or anything that would push that statement into too much for her.

Alyssa was the one blushing now. The idea of spending the next week and maybe even more time with him sounded fabulous, but sadly it scared her too. She'd loved spending time with Tyler until he pushed himself on her and she had to find a way home in a foreign country. She focused on Beck and some of her reservations melted away. "I *think* I could spare some time for you, but maybe you want to find A. A. and try to convince him."

"A.A. was just some initials. You're Alyssa. Beautiful, talented, and fun, and hopefully if I play my cards right, the woman who'll be traveling the world with me and rescuing children along the way."

He grinned and Alyssa almost told him right then she'd pack her bags, but her usual caution with men held her back. What did she really know about Beckham Taylor? It was time for some Maryn type research and in the meantime, she'd get to know him and make an informed decision. Unfortunately, her eyes strayed to his lips and she found herself hoping he'd convince her in ways that had nothing to do with trusting a man's character or furthering children's charities.

The pizza arrived and Alyssa didn't have to give him a response. She wondered if this was a dream opportunity or just another business proposition from a wealthy man who thought he could buy anything he wanted, including her. A shiver of terror went down her spine as she couldn't quite forget the men her father used to push on her. Men like Joel, Tyler, Hugh and others who she'd successfully removed from her memory. Men who assumed she would want them because they were wealthy or because her father tried to sell her to the highest bidder. She was a free woman now and definitely not for sale, but maybe Beckham could convince her to be his photographer. With that smile, he just might.

Chapter Eight

Alyssa escaped to the pool area. She couldn't handle one more leering look from her father's "friends." Especially Hugh. He made her skin crawl with his shirt unbuttoned to his belly button, exposing nasty dark hair and more gold chains than any self-respecting man should ever wear. She giggled at herself. No man should wear gold chains.

She sobered quickly and shook her head. Teach her to ever believe her dad's stories. He'd begged her to come to dinner tonight, claiming her mom missed her so much she was making herself ill. What a crock. She'd barely seen her mother before this group of disgusting men had descended on the house. What was her dad promising them? He was such a slime ball.

Arms snaked around her stomach. Alyssa squeaked and dropped her drink. The glass shattered, spraying her legs with shards of crystal, ice, and water.

"I knew you'd find a way to get me alone," a voice said in her ear as too-soft lips nuzzled her neck. "I've seen you eyeing me all night."

"Let me go," Alyssa demanded, straining against his grip.

He whirled her to face him, but didn't loosen his hold. It was Hugh. Oh, no. He was grinning at her like she was the prime rib. Gross.

"Don't worry, love, I won't hurt you. Just want a little taste of this... beauty." He leaned closer. His breath reeked. Alcohol and fish. He must love oysters. She was going to be sick.

Alyssa was able to free her hand and smack him hard across the face. "Get away from me!"

Hugh grabbed both of her arms and squeezed. "That's no way to treat a prospective buyer."

59

"What?" she managed, gasping from the fear of what he would do and the pain in her biceps.

"Don't play stupid. It doesn't fit you." His hot, foul breath brushed her cheek as he leaned in.

"I have no clue what you're talking about, but my father is going to be livid if you don't release me." She strained against his grip but it was like iron. Sadly, she knew her threat was empty. Her father had made it clear years ago how she was supposed to behave around his friends.

"Your father. Ha!" Hugh chuckled heartily. "Your beloved father is the one who put you up for sale. My buddies and I came here tonight to preview our beautiful piece of livestock. I think it's worth a lot." He tried to pull her close.

Alyssa spit in his face. His eyes hardened and he released one of her arms and grabbed the collar of her blouse. One rip and it shredded in his hands. "Now that's more like it." He grunted and grabbed her breast.

Raising her right knee, she felt her bones impact his disgusting softness and almost recoiled but instead used every ounce of leg strength to make him hurt.

Hugh gasped and his grip weakened.

Alyssa tore herself away.

"I will buy you," Hugh groaned out.

Alyssa sprang awake in her bed.

She looked around, trying to get her bearings. She was in Hawaii. Hugh and her dad were nowhere around. She fell against the pillows, her tears hot against her cheeks, hoping she'd never have to face the nightmare or her father again.

Alyssa's phone rang as she was re-packing her camera. Beck had asked if he could take them to lunch and Granny was still sleeping even though it was late morning. Alyssa had been relieved to have time to shake off the recurring dream in the bright sunshine. The nightmare didn't come as often anymore, but it always played almost verbatim. The attempted rape was horrid, but the worst part was knowing how twisted her father's mind was. He'd always told her he would "take care of her" she just hadn't fully comprehended he meant to do it by selling her to one of his friends and thinking that they'd all be one happy family. No, thank you.

She'd enjoyed her walk around the neighborhood with her camera this morning, searching for new shots. Luckily, the boys were up to their Ripstiking antics and she'd gotten some fabulous shots of them teaching the younger children in the neighborhood.

"Hello," she said when the phone trumpeted again, she really needed to change that.

"How's the reclusive Richie?" Maryn smacked her lips like she was kissing the phone.

"He's a good guy," Alyssa admitted. She walked onto her balcony and looked at the lush trees in the bed and breakfast's yard. It would be hard to leave a place where papaya grew on the trees. It seemed absurd to not be thrilled with the opportunity to take a world-wide trip with a man as kind, wealthy, and good-looking as Beck, but because of past trauma with men she had a lot of reservations about committing, especially after a repeat of Hugh's attack in her sleep. Added to that was the worry of how to tell Beck about the pictures she'd taken of him and his sister.

"Is that all?" Maryn prodded.

"So far he's been nothing but the perfect gentleman," Alyssa admitted. Beck seemed like everything her teenage self used to fantasize about, but she was all grown up now and reality was often very different than pipe dreams.

"Any lip action or proposals?"

"No lip action." Alyssa paused. What did Maryn know? Had she been privy to what Beck was planning and not clued her in? "Did you know he was going to ask me to be his photographer?"

"His *photographer*? Heck, no. I meant proposals of marriage, you dork."

"Oh." Alyssa was relieved that her friend hadn't been hiding anything.

"He asked you to photograph, what? His hotness? That wouldn't be a bad job. You promised me pics two days ago and I'm still waiting. The photos I have in his file look like he's pretty well-built."

"He's definitely well-built." Alyssa smiled, remembering his reluctance to take his shirt off and loving that they shared insecurities about their imperfections. But unlike her foot, his chest was beautiful, even with the scars. "He wants me to travel with him and photograph children in underdeveloped countries to help raise awareness for their needs."

"You're going on a world-wide trip with *Beckham Taylor*?" Maryn squealed in delight. "Oh, yeah, I hooked my girl up. Oh, yeah, she's going to marry a stinking billionaire."

"Maryn," Alyssa interrupted, trying hard not to laugh. "I didn't agree to go. I'm the dark side of the billionaire bride pact, remember? All the other girls admitted I was least likely to ever fulfill the stupid pact." Curse Erin for instigating the pact and Alyssa for ever agreeing. Well, she couldn't quite curse Erin, her friend was amazing and too genuine to be cursed.

"What? I didn't raise you to be a fool."

"Now you sound like Granny."

"Good. She'd agree with me."

Alyssa hadn't said anything to Granny yet. She would definitely agree with Maryn.

"Come on, sis. When an opportunity like this comes up, you jump on it, or him, as the case may be."

Alyssa blushed at the image of her jumping into Beck's arms. Oh, my. She fanned herself with her hand. The outside breeze wasn't enough. "I'm just giving myself some time to think it all through. I told him I'd get back to him at the end of the week."

"So you didn't say no?"

"Not yet."

"And he's spending quality time with you all week to convince you to go?"

"Oh, I hope so."

Maryn laughed. "That's more like it."

"Hey," Alyssa interrupted Maryn's chortling laughter. "Can you do some research for me?"

"On what?"

"Him."

"Come on. At some point you have to learn to trust a man without delving into every speck of dirt he's ever rolled in."

"Please." Alyssa picked at a hangnail and lowered her voice, "You know how it is for me."

Maryn sighed. "Sorry, sis. I keep praying you'll get past it all."

"I had the nightmare again last night."

"Oh. Sorry I wasn't there."

"Me too." Maryn used to wake her from the nightmare when Alyssa cried out in her sleep. It was always a relief to not have to play the entire episode out and have somebody to talk to about it. "Maybe someday it'll stop." She thought of Beck and wondered if spending more time with him might stop the terrifying dream.

"I know you'll do a great job of researching," she said to Maryn, "and I really need to know what I'm getting into here. I want to be able to trust him."

"Trust isn't earned by a squeaky clean background."

"It isn't going to hurt though."

Maryn sighed. "Fine. I'll do it. Your main concern?"

"You know me. How has he treated the women in his life? Does he think being wealthy gives him the right to take anything he wants?"

"I'll see what I can find but honestly, Alyssa, you need to do your own research. How does he make you feel? How does he treat Granny? The waitress? The little girl on the street? Trust yourself and maybe you can learn to trust a man."

Alyssa soaked the words in. Maryn had been her best friend for long enough she only had her best interests at heart. "But-but... what if he finds out I took those pictures of him after his parents' funeral?"

Maryn inhaled sharply. "Deal with that when you get there. It's okay to allow yourself to have fun, to open up the possibility of having a relationship with a good guy. Don't let your guilt or your dad's manipulation ruin the rest of your life." She paused as if waiting for Alyssa to respond. When Alyssa didn't, she prompted. "Right?"

Alyssa gripped onto the railing with her left hand and the phone with her right. Was Beck a good guy? Was she willing to get to know him and find out? "Right," Alyssa finally admitted.

"Love us," Maryn said.

Alyssa laughed. Years ago, Alyssa had texted "love ya" to Maryn but it had auto-corrected to "love us". Maryn loved to tease her about it, but it had become a sort of mantra for them and Alyssa truly did love them, their friendship, their closeness, she'd be lost without Maryn.

"Love us too." Alyssa hung up the phone and closed her eyes, letting the gentle breeze caress her face. Could she trust a man? She pictured Beck's blue eyes sparkling at her. Maybe.

Chapter Nine

Alyssa was excited to try out Pa'ia's Fish Market for lunch. Jerry claimed they had the best fish tacos he'd ever eaten in his life, but she hadn't stopped on her travels around the island to see if she agreed. Beck, Alyssa, and Granny drove the thirty minutes to the center of the island and found a parking lot a couple blocks behind the restaurant. Beck hurried around and opened Alyssa and Granny's doors at the same time. Alyssa stepped out of the car and glimpsed a man, with hair so blond it was almost white, duck into a Lexus sport utility a few cars down. She frowned and shook her head. It couldn't be, but it had looked so much like him.

"Granny," she whispered, leaning close. "Do you know where Dad is right now?"

Granny shook her head, her blue eyes darkening. "I try not to keep up with him."

Alyssa looked back at the Lexus, but there was no more movement. Instead a group of scrubby young men lounging on the grass next to the parking lot drew her gaze.

"Hi, pretty lady," a guy with dreadlocks called out to Alyssa. "You want to take a drag of my bong with me?"

"No, thank you," Alyssa said.

Beck stepped protectively in front of her.

"What's a bong?" Granny asked.

"It's the pipe you use to smoke marijuana," Beck said quietly.

"Isn't that illegal here?" Alyssa asked. She'd only driven through

Pa'ia to get to the scenic road to Hana for photo shoots, but she'd heard of other tourists being offered drugs in the small town.

"Yeah."

Granny's eyes widened. She stepped deftly around Beck and came at the young man who had spoken to Alyssa with her purse held high. "What are you doing wasting your life like this?" She smacked him on the arm with her purse.

"Ouch!" He scowled and scooted away on the grass.

Beck hurried to Granny's side, taking her arm and having to almost drag her away.

"Get a job and get off the sauce," Granny yelled as they hurried to the sidewalk. She straightened her blouse and glared at Beck. "Let me go. I won't smack him again."

"Granny," Alyssa said, looking over her shoulder at the young man, who studied her with an intensity that frightened her. "He could've hurt you."

"Ha. I'm tougher than that loser." They walked past a custard shop and Granny got distracted. "Can we go there after the fish tacos? Ooh, I love that stuff."

"Sure." Beck smiled and shrugged at Alyssa.

"I'm never sure what to do with young people who are wasting their lives," Granny admitted. "Do they need more love or a kick in the pants? That one seemed like he needed several kicks."

Beck laughed. "It's a struggle knowing how to respond."

Granny tilted her head up to give him a glacial stare. "Just you wait, someday you'll have children and you'll know exactly what I mean. Now that I look back I should've loved Gary, Alyssa's dad, more. But at the time I was so frustrated, the kick in the butt was the only way I knew how to respond."

A cloud passed over the sun, reflecting the darkness seeping into Alyssa. Granny always tried to take the blame for how Alyssa's dad acted, but Alyssa didn't buy it. The man was born manipulating and had tried to bully her and every one she knew her entire life.

"Excuse me," Alyssa muttered as they walked into the open doors of the restaurant. "I need to find a restroom."

Beck asked an employee and retrieved the restroom key.

"Would you like me to order for you?" Beck asked. His eyes said he knew exactly why she was escaping, but was too kind to ask.

"Yes, please. The fish tacos sound great." She gave him an empty smile and walked away. The employee gestured her around the back of the restaurant to a small dirt-packed alley. At the very end of the alleyway it curved and finally there was a restroom sign on a beat up metal door.

Alyssa thought she wanted a minute alone, but the isolation of the bathroom and the whole feel of this town creeped her out. She quickly splashed some water on her face, reapplied lip balm, and exited the dirty bathroom.

The young man with dreadlocks stood right outside the door.

"Oh!" Alyssa's eyes darted to his face then away. He was tall and broad-shouldered. She tried to go around him, but he grabbed her arm. "Excuse me," she said, her voice icy.

"Have you done something I need to excuse?" He smirked at her. His eyes were a bit cloudy, but focused on her. He didn't appear to be too out of it from the drugs.

"I need to get back to my date before he comes looking for me." Even as she said it, she knew Beck would give her all the time she needed. He seemed to understand how much the mention of her dad had upset her.

"I think we've got a few minutes." The man yanked on her arm and brought her into full contact with his body. She tripped on her bad foot and landed hard against his chest. "Now that's more like it."

He stunk like the too-sweet smell of marijuana. Alyssa gagged and tried to pull free, digging into his arm with the restroom key. He yanked the key from her hand and tossed it.

"Oh, no, pretty lady. We're going to have some fun." His scruffy face descended to within inches of hers.

Alyssa ducked her head and yanked to free her arms. She brought her knee up, but only succeeded in hitting him in the thigh with it.

"A fighter? I like it."

No, no, no. This couldn't be happening to her again. How could she get away? She strained against his strong grip, but he grabbed her hair and yanked her head back. Alyssa screamed and then spit in his face. He didn't even wipe the spittle away, just chuckled and pulled her closer.

"Let's see if you taste as good as you look." He pressed his mouth to hers, trying to force her mouth open with his tongue.

He tasted awful. Alyssa clamped her teeth tightly so he couldn't gain access to her mouth. She squirmed and pushed, but couldn't free herself. The tight clasp he had on her hair was giving her a headache, but his disgusting lips covering her mouth was worse.

Suddenly, he was yanked backwards. His grip on her loosened, but he still pulled Alyssa with him. Alyssa grabbed onto the door handle and steadied herself as he was dragged away. Alyssa wiped the foul taste of him from her mouth and looked up to see Beck throw the guy to the ground.

"Beck," she breathed.

He rushed to her side and wrapped his arm around her. "You okay?"

"Um..." She really wasn't sure. Her heart raced, her palms were sweaty, and she couldn't catch a full breath.

The guy slammed his fist into Beck's back. Beck grunted, a look of surprise crossing his face. Alyssa jumped. She hadn't even seen him coming. Beck turned to face the guy and with several well-placed jabs knocked him back to the dirt-packed alley. The guy growled and pushed off the ground, driving his head into Beck's abdomen. Beck swept his feet out from under him and the guy went down hard again. Beck had half a grin on his face as he waited for the guy to recover so he could hit him again.

"Not worth it," the druggie muttered. Shaking his head as if to clear it, he staggered to his feet and scurried away.

Beck turned back to Alyssa.

"Wow," she said, offering him half a smile. She took several slow breaths and tried to control her trembling hands. "Where did you learn how to fight like that?"

"Hockey." He released his clenched fists and blew out a breath before giving her a chagrined smile. "I spent a lot of time in the penalty box."

Alyssa laughed. A euphoria of freedom rushed through her. She was safe. She was okay. It felt so good to think those thoughts after the terror of being trapped and kissed by the druggie. "Thanks for coming for me."

Beck wrapped his arms around her waist. It was completely natural to grip his strong shoulders in her hands, to want to pull him close instead of push him away.

"I saw that guy walk by a few minutes ago," Beck said. "He looked into the restaurant and smirked at me and Granny. It hit me that he was up to no good, and then I heard your scream."

Alyssa couldn't control the shudder that raced through her. Beck had rescued her. The last time she'd succeeded in escaping after she kneed Hugh. She found out later he hadn't chased her because he planned to pay her dad for her. He thought she would marry him because of her dad forcing her hand. She'd run away from her parent's home and never looked back. Sadly, she hadn't trusted a man since that day either. Why was Beck so different?

Beck nestled her against his chest and rested his cheek on her hair. "I'm sorry he touched you."

"Thank you for your help." She fought hard but couldn't control the tremble in her voice.

"Anytime."

"You could help some more," she whispered, amazed at the comfort and excitement of Beck's arms.

Beck lifted his head and stared down into her eyes. "How?"

"Replace the awful taste of him trying to kiss me." Oh, my heavens. Alyssa had just said that, and she truly wanted his kiss more than she could express.

Beck's smile crinkled his cheeks and warmed his blue eyes. "Gladly."

He lowered his head and gently took possession of her mouth. She ran her hands up his back, entangling her fingers in his hair. He tasted like peppermint and the world seemed to spin as her lips tingled from his caress.

"Is she okay?" Granny's voice came from around the building. "Oh! Excuse me."

They broke apart to see Granny scurrying quickly away. Alyssa laughed. "She would not have wanted to interrupt this moment."

"I wanted our first kiss to be somewhere romantic," Beck said, trailing his fingers down her cheek.

Alyssa looked around the dirty alley and laughed. "I asked you for the kiss, so it's my fault it wasn't a romantic setting."

"You make it romantic, Alyssa," Beck said and then they were kissing again. His lips were every bit as well-formed as she'd imagined. They caressed hers with such tenderness and just the right amount of pressure. Her body flushed with excitement and pleasure.

Alyssa enjoyed each second of Beck's touch and kiss. She finally forced herself to break away. "We're giving Granny too much pleasure here," she whispered.

"I thought it was me that was having too much pleasure," Beck said with a wink and a look that warmed her almost as much as his touch.

Beck wrapped an arm around her waist and escorted her back to Granny. They called the police and reported the attack, but the officer they talked to wasn't very encouraging. He said the guy's description fit a lot of the local population in Pa'ia. He promised to get back to them if he found anything.

Beck ordered their fish tacos to go and they drove away from Pa'ia as fast as they could. Granny alternated between concern for Alyssa and a self-satisfied grin as she looked back and forth between the two of them. Alyssa wished Granny hadn't witnessed their first kiss, she would never hear the end of it. Yet at the same time, she didn't really mind because as long as she stayed close to Beck, she felt safe. It was the first time in her life that a man had done that for her.

Chapter Ten

Ever since Alyssa first moved to Maui, she had wanted to go on a snorkeling excursion around the small island of Lanai, but she didn't like the idea of going by herself. She couldn't bring her expensive camera and risk it getting wet, so she couldn't justify the expense of a snorkeling trip or use it as a tax write-off. She made the mistake of mentioning her desire to Beck and Granny at lunch and Beck immediately found the phone number and bought tickets for the next morning.

Beck and Alyssa arrived at the dock and smiled greetings to the dozen other people milling around the jet boat. After some fruit, granola bars, and instructions from Captain Aaron, they waited until Aaron's assistant guided the boat into the water then walked down the dock and climbed in. Everyone was instructed to take off their shoes. Alyssa followed suit, telling herself that she didn't know these people and didn't care if they saw her deformed foot. She straddled the inflatable side of the boat, flinching when Captain Aaron gunned the boat. They skimmed across the water, and the chilly ocean spray hit her leg.

"Cold?" Beck asked, his mouth next to her ear.

"A little," she admitted. "I'm usually running this time of day, not getting ready to jump in the water."

Beck chuckled and scooted up behind her, wrapping his arms around her waist.

The warmth and excitement of his touch were exactly what she needed to forget the cold. She leaned back against his muscular chest and he tightened his hold on her. She loved the intimacy and warmth of his arms. She could almost believe they were a couple and Beck would always be there to shield her with his strength from the cold or whatever else life threw at her.

It was over an hour boat ride to the island of Lanai, but Alyssa hardly noticed as she savored Beck's touch and laughed at the cute antics of a seven-year old red-headed boy, Stockton. His parents obviously adored him, but were also beside themselves as they tried to contain him from running around in the boat, talking to everyone, and almost launching himself into the ocean a dozen times. He and Alyssa instantly bonded as he discovered that the Denver Broncos were her favorite NFL football team.

"I'm gonna play wide receiver for them someday," Stockton informed her. "Do you wanna see how fast I can run?"

"Yes." Alyssa grabbed him around the waist as he tried to take off at a sprint. "But let's wait until we're on the ground."

Stockton's mother, Janie, smiled her thanks as the little boy squirmed from Alyssa's arms.

Captain Aaron maneuvered the boat next to an interesting World War II battleship that had run aground on the island. Alyssa imagined the stories that massive iron hull could tell.

They continued on their journey and saw whales, dolphins, and sea turtles. The boat stopped just offshore of a sandy beach. "Time for your first swim of the day," Captain Aaron announced.

Alyssa straightened. "Is he crazy? I'm still half-frozen."

The brochure had bragged about walking on a white sand, private beach and apparently this was that opportunity. Alyssa had walked on a lot of nice beaches and was tempted to stay in the boat and wait for the snorkeling.

Beck rubbed his hands down her arms. "Guess my hug didn't help?"

"Oh, it helped." She smiled, grateful and a little surprised at how comfortable she was with him. She'd thought of little last night but his kiss and his offer to travel with him. She felt like she'd be an idiot not to go. If they kept getting as close over the next few days, she'd have no choice but to go, or experience withdrawals from being around him. "But I'd rather hug you than jump in that water right now."

Beck stood and offered her a hand. "And here I thought you were an adventurous girl."

Alyssa arched an eyebrow. She knew a challenge when she heard one. Pulling off her sweatshirt and then her swimsuit cover up, she leapt over the side and into the water. The cold liquid closed over her head and she gasped, swallowing a mouthful of water. Alyssa swam toward the surface, coughing and spitting as she hit the air.

Beck was by her side. "You okay?"

"Y-yes." She coughed a few more times then started stroking toward the island. "I decided to taste the water. A bit too salty."

Beck chuckled and swam close by her side. They quickly reached the island and enjoyed walking in the soft sand and exploring. It reminded Alyssa of the spots she'd read about in books where someone is shipwrecked on a deserted island—sandy beach with trees and vegetation above that looked like a jungle. She glanced up at Beck's handsome face and wished they were alone on this beautiful spot.

Beck must've been feeling the same way. His grip on her hand tightened and he tugged her behind a palm tree. He smiled and trailed his fingertips lightly down the side of her face. Alyssa moistened her lips and stepped closer, waiting, hoping. She closed her eyes, savoring his soft touch as he tilted her chin up.

"Hey, Lyssa," Stockton yelled. "I found shells! Lyssa. Where are you?"

Alyssa felt disappointment instead of Beck's lips. He cleared his throat and then escorted her around the tree.

"Hey! I didn't know you and Beck were hiding. Look at my shells," Stockton said.

She and Beck walked over to the little boy and inspected his treasures. His dad, Bryant, gave Beck an apologetic smile. "Sorry, he's kind of insistent."

"He's great," Beck said. "No worries."

Beck ran a hand through his hair and Alyssa liked that his frustration was evident, not at Stockton, but at the missed opportunity.

Stockton's mom beamed at her son. Alyssa didn't blame her. The little guy was so cute she couldn't find it in her to be upset that he'd interrupted their privacy. Alyssa glanced at Beck and he met her eye. She wondered what their son would look like. Blood rushed to her cheeks. What kind of a thought was that? She liked Beck, a lot, but she wasn't ready for some lifelong commitment. She quickly looked away and shuffled her abnormal right foot through the sand.

Captain Aaron called them back to the boat a few minutes later. The swim back felt refreshing instead of freezing. They cruised farther around the island and went to several different snorkeling spots, stopping for lunch next to some water-filled caves. Alyssa's favorite snorkeling spot was a huge rock island that they swam around numerous times, staring at thousands of brightly-colored fish. Glancing at the wide expanse of ocean around her, she had the brief, and hopefully completely irrational, fear of a shark appearing.

She should've never watched Soul Surfer. Wasn't that filmed in Hawaii? She found herself wondering what island. Was it Kauai or Maui? Shaking her head, she concentrated on the picturesque ocean spread beneath her.

She was kicking hard for another pass when she felt a tug on her arm. She turned to see Beck motioning and pulling her toward the boat. She lifted her head out of the water.

"Shark," he said, giving her a push toward the boat.

"No!" she gargled through her mask. Darting a glance over her shoulder, she saw the fin about twenty yards away. Alyssa kicked as hard as she could toward the boat, expecting any second to feel the shark's teeth tearing into her. Her right foot throbbed from trying to keep it in the flipper correctly, but she couldn't quit. Her chest constricted and she cried out inside her mask. She couldn't get enough air. Spitting the mouthpiece out, she wanted to look, but forced herself to stay focused on reaching the boat.

Please, please, keep us all safe, she prayed over and over again.

Something brushed against her leg. She screamed and jerked away, certain the shark was right next to her and would rip her apart. Turning, relief rushed through her when she realized it was Beck swimming next to her. He'd inserted his body between her and the shark. The fin was coming closer and Alyssa continued to pray for their protection.

The ladder appeared and Captain Aaron's hand. Beck pushed her up from behind and she scrambled into the boat, Beck right behind her. She wrapped up in the towel that Aaron's assistant handed her.

"Is everyone in?" Beck asked over her shoulder.

"Stockton, Janie, and Bryant are on the other side of the island," Aaron said, already putting the motor into motion and cruising around the rock.

"Is that a great white?" Aaron's assistant asked, sounding almost excited.

"Yes," Aaron replied, expertly spinning the wheel. "They travel here in the winter months."

Alyssa searched the water and saw the tell-tale fin moving parallel to them in the ocean. She thanked her father in heaven for her and Beck's safety and continued praying hard that they could get to the little family before the shark decided to attack. Could they scare it away somehow? They rounded the island and the three snorkels were right there in the water.

Someone screamed and Alyssa saw the shark's speed had increased. Aaron positioned the boat between the shark and the family. Alyssa breathed a sigh of relief until she noticed the shark slowed and then veered around the boat.

Bryant, Stockton's dad, jerked his head out of the water.

"Shark!" several people screamed. He shoved his wife toward the boat. She looked up, confused, but responded to Beck's outstretched arm and was pulled quickly to safety. Cute little Stockton was completely oblivious to the approaching danger and had his head down. He'd been so intrigued by the fish and was probably focused on them. His dad reached for him, but wasn't close enough. Alyssa cried out in panic as the shark sliced through the water toward the little boy. Beck picked up an oxygen tank and hurled it at the approaching shark. It bounced off the shark and barely missed Bryant.

Stockton finally looked up from the water and screamed in surprise. The shark was temporarily thrown off course and Aaron had managed to get the boat close enough for Beck to lean over and pluck Stockton from the water. He ushered him into his mother's waiting arms and turned around to help Bryant. Bryant started scrambling up the ladder with Beck yanking on him. The shark swam toward the boat.

Alyssa panted for air. It was a scene out of a horror movie, and Bryant was about to become a real-life victim. Captain Aaron threw the motor into gear. Beck flew over the side of the boat and toward the waiting jaws of the shark. The screams and shouts of panic pressed in around Alyssa. She knew she was screaming louder than anyone, but she felt like everything was frozen except the boat and that horrible shark coming straight for Beck.

Bryant darted back down the ladder and reached out a hand. Beck grabbed onto him and hung on. A sharp tug from Bryant and Beck was able to secure a leg around the ladder and pull himself up. The boat flew away from the shark as Beck clung onto the ladder next to Bryant. Bryant climbed the remaining steps and then helped Beck over the side.

Alyssa hurried to Beck's side, flinging herself at him. They sank down into the cushions at the back of the boat. She hugged him and couldn't stop the tears racing down her face.

"Oh, Beck, you're okay."

Janie made her way to them with Stockton hanging on her. "You saved us," she said. "Thank you."

Bryant nodded, offering his hand. "I owe you everything."

"You saved me too," Beck said, shaking Bryant's hand.

"You're both heroes in my book," Captain Aaron added, turning around to give them both a salute. "Maybe the pretty lady can give you a reward for all of us." He winked at Alyssa and Beck.

Alyssa kissed Beck right in front of everybody. The boat exploded in cheers and she pulled away in embarrassment.

"Mommy, I want ice cream for a reward for being brave, not a kiss from Lyssa," Stockton said.

Beck grinned at the little boy. "When we get back, buddy, I'll buy you ice cream, and I'll take all your kisses from Lyssa."

Alyssa enjoyed the salty taste of the ocean as Beck proceeded to kiss her again and her heart thumped in excitement that had nothing to do with sharks or near-death experiences.

Beck escorted Alyssa off the boat and they took their time saying goodbye to the group. The shark attack had bonded everyone together. Stockton was still insistent that he didn't want kisses, but he did accept a hug from Alyssa after Beck found an ice cream shop and bought them both an ice cream.

"You sure you don't want a lick?" Alyssa asked, her tongue drawing patterns in the chocolate-chocolate chip ice cream.

Beck might've drooled a little bit. "A lick of what?"

"The ice cream, you silly." Her face reddened. "I look awful." She tried to fluff her hair, but spending the day in the ocean had it plastered to her head.

"You look great," Beck reassured her and he meant it. He'd never seen his former girlfriend, Belle, without makeup so thick she must have applied it with a painter's trowel. Alyssa didn't need makeup to look beautiful. He hadn't realized how much he'd dreamed of finding a woman who was not only beautiful but genuine. Alyssa didn't have an agenda where he was concerned and she wasn't selfish and manipulative.

His phone rang. He checked the caller I.D. before saying to Alyssa, "Excuse me, I need to take this."

She nodded her understanding.

"Hey, Linli. You doing okay without me?" Beck asked.

"Of course." Linli huffed and he knew he'd offended her. She could and did run the office without any help from him and it irritated her when he acted like he helped out. "But I have to tell you, Beck, I'm more certain than ever that somebody took your itinerary and I'm afraid it's Belle."

"Belle?" His voice pitched up in surprise.

Alyssa looked at him strangely and he tried to smile like nothing was wrong.

"You don't think she'd come here?" he asked more quietly.

"I wouldn't put it past her. The woman thinks she owns you."

"She knows we're just friends."

Linli harrumphed and Alyssa's eyebrows rose.

"Okay. Thanks for the heads up, boss."

"You'd better remember who the boss is. Stay safe. It might not be her. It could be anyone—gold diggers, photographers, or any other kind of horrible people like that."

"Photographers?"

Alyssa took a step back, not licking her ice cream any more. Beck shook his head and smiled like his assistant was crazy.

"You know how they are, trying to take pictures of you in your skivvies and disgusting stuff like that. Just be careful."

A chill ran through him at her warning. He looked at Alyssa. She was a photographer, but a beautiful and considerate kind of photographer. She'd never take unwanted pictures of someone for profit. Her talent was a gift to the world, not smutty pictures for the tabloids.

"Thanks, Linli," he said to his assistant.

"It's what I do." Linli hung up before he could say goodbye.

"Everything okay?" Alyssa asked.

"Yeah. My assistant is a bit paranoid. She thinks someone stole my itinerary and is trying to exploit me."

Alyssa swallowed and stared at him. A chocolate drip ran over the back of her hand.

"Don't worry. I'll be fine. There's nothing the tabloid rags can do to me that they haven't already done." He thought of the pictures taken after his parents' funeral. They'd twisted a situation with his sister, Anna, and made it look like he was restraining her and then she was hitting him, when in truth he'd been holding her as she sobbed and then she'd accidentally elbowed him when they both bent to pick up her son. To think that someone had intruded on their grief and made them fodder for gossip, that was completely untrue, still upset him sometimes.

"Oh, um, okay." A panicked look filled her eyes and the ice cream was still dripping down her hand.

Beck smiled to reassure her then the realization occurred to him. "You're worried they're going to photograph us together."

"Oh, no, it's fine." She shook her head quickly, failing to convince him. She was famous in her own right. Of course she wouldn't want some smart tabloid writer to piece together that A.A. was with Beckham Taylor and though he was thrilled to be with her, he didn't want his private life on display, ever.

"It's not fine. We'll watch out for them." He wrapped an arm around her then took her napkin and wiped her hand off.

Alyssa giggled, but she still sounded nervous. He'd better get her back to the bed and breakfast. It had been a long day and she was probably exhausted. He regretted saying anything to her about the photographers. A true artist like her would never understand those cockroaches who stooped to exploit others and sell hurtful pictures to the tabloids.

Chapter Eleven

"I have a clean report for one Beck-ham Taylor," Maryn drawled out.

Alyssa sank onto her bed. "Really?" Was her intuition finally on? Beck was a good guy and wouldn't hurt her? Her heart raced as she thought of Beck's exciting kisses in the boat today but then it dropped when she remembered the intense scorn he'd shown for the paparazzi. How could she ever tell him she'd been desperate enough to do that, and even worse, to take pictures of him and his family when they were grieving? She hadn't known how far the tabloid would twist the pictures she'd taken, but still it made her physically sick.

"Yep. He's a good guy, my friend, committed to his family and helping children. Of course there were some pictures of him dating, but it was never smutty or anything."

"Maryn," Alyssa all but wailed, "How am I going to tell him I took those pictures of him and his sister?"

"I don't know, sweets. Maybe give it a little more time. No reason to unload all the dirt on the second date."

"I feel like I'm hiding something from him." Alyssa pressed her eyes closed. "I hate it."

"That's because you're so pure and good. Take your time and get to know him. When he sees how sweet you are, he'll know my girl would never take advantage of anyone, and he won't care what you've done in the past."

Alyssa sighed. "Thank you, friend, that means a lot to me."

"It's true. So tell me... you got a scoop?"

"You had better be kidding." Alyssa hated the way Maryn had phrased that. She stretched out on her bed and pressed the phone to her ear. "No more scoops. I told you about the first day we spent together. You said nothing else was going to get printed in that stupid article and you promised no names."

"Of course, no more scoops, like that kind of scoops, unless we're talking about ice cream." Maryn laughed. "I just love hearing about your romance."

"Yeah, yeah, sadly I know you too well to believe that." Beck had been so thoughtful to buy her and Stockton ice cream and the look in his eyes as he wiped it off her hand... Was Maryn right that he'd understand or was he going to hate her?

"Hey, I'm offended by that calloused remark. This is all best buddy here, off the record. I already promised not to write any of this, but you have to give me some dirt. Any lip action happening yet?"

Alyssa let out her breath on a whispered sigh. She pointed her toes and enjoyed being lazy and thinking about Beck's kisses. Maryn was right, it was smarter to wait and get to know Beck better before she stressed over revealing all her secrets. "It was amazing."

"Now that's more like it. I'm demanding best friend rights, describe, please."

"Which time?"

"Oh, yeah! Loving that. First time then we can get all the grit later."

Alyssa laughed. "All I can say is he rescued me from some druggie, and then he completely took my breath away."

"Ah, that's beautiful. So, you're really liking this guy?"

"Yes."

"And you really appreciate your best friend setting this all up?"

"Yes." Alyssa was wary again. "But you already owe me twenty favors so I'm not doing anything more for you."

"I'm hurt! I just wanted to hear your gratitude."

"I am grateful. He's one of the best men I've ever met."

"See, that's all I wanted. Now go find him and kiss him some more, and I expect you to name your first daughter after me."

Alyssa hung up the phone with a smile. Maryn *was* a cute name for a little girl. She laughed. She was getting more than a little ahead of herself. Alyssa was one of the few from their group of twelve who regretted making the Billionaire Bride Pact at twelve years old. As Maryn liked to tease her, Alyssa was the dark side of the pact. She really had no desire to marry a Richie. She smiled, but Beck was so much more than some rich guy. He didn't act anything like her father or all the men her father had tried to push on her over the years.

She opened her computer, to try and stop her daydreams and worries over Beck, and started sorting the pictures she'd taken of the village of Nahiku last week. A local had taken her there, otherwise she would've been met with hostility as a tourist. A popular tourist book recommended people explore the village, but the locals wanted their privacy. When tourists appeared, it was an awkward situation at best, sometimes even resulting in arguments or attacks on the tourists.

The villagers had welcomed her with open arms, partially because of Jerry's friend who took her, and partially because her dark coloring helped her to fit in. The beautiful village brought such a sense of another era of time. A simple life where children played in the streets without fear and laughed unabashedly because they were loved by family and neighbors alike. Alyssa had never experienced that feeling.

She heard a rap on her door and her heartbeat immediately quickened, hoping it might be Beck. She swung the door open wide. Beck leaned against the frame. Her breath hitched at the warmth in his blue eyes and for the first time in longer than she could remember, she wasn't afraid to have a man standing outside her room. She could invite him in and not worry that he would try to seduce or attack her. Though she might not mind if Beck tried to seduce her.

"Do you want to go for a walk?"

She glanced down at the sweats and raggedy T-shirt she'd thrown on after her shower. "I look horrible."

He shook his head. "You look beautiful."

She blushed. "At least it's dark outside."

He smiled and offered his arm. She quickly slipped on her tennis shoes and tied them, then grasped his elbow. They walked down the street to the beach and sauntered slowly along. Beck stopped by the rocks before Canoe Beach and turned to face her.

"I hear there are turtles here in the mornings."

"There are. I see them on my runs all the time."

Alyssa's breath came hard and fast. From the look in his eyes, he didn't bring her here to talk about turtles. She was grateful he hadn't bugged her about her decision to travel with him and photograph either. He was so respectful and kind, giving her time to sort things out. Now if she could just get brave enough to tell him about the photographs she'd taken. Despite Maryn's reassurance, she was afraid that the longer she waited, the worse it was going to be.

Beck smiled and brushed a lock of hair from her face. He slowly lowered his head, but paused and whispered, "Alyssa?" as if asking permission.

She nodded and that must've been all the answer he needed. He took command of her lips with a passion that heated her all the way through. She relished each movement of his lips and the way his hands massaged her back in rhythm with the kiss. Every nerve tingled and her head filled up with only Beck.

He broke contact and asked, "Was that a bit more romantic than the alley of a bathroom or a boat with a dozen people watching?"

She laughed. "When you kiss me, I'm not even sure where I am, so I really don't think the setting matters."

He grinned and lowered his head to hers again.

Chapter Twelve

Alyssa looked at the monstrous waves off the northwestern point of the island. Surfers were scattered throughout the water, working to catch a big wave. She secured her camera bag over her shoulder and swung back to face Beck as he eased the surfboard off the top of his rental car. "Do you have a death wish?"

Beck laughed and gestured down to the water. "These are small waves."

"Suicidal," Alyssa muttered, the shark attack still fresh in her mind. It would be a few days before she got back in the water.

"I promise I'll be safe."

Beck rested the surfboard against the car and pulled his T-shirt off. Alyssa lost the ability to disagree with him as she studied the well-defined lines of his chest. The scars saddened her as she hated to think of Beck being in pain, but they added to his appeal. He was a fierce warrior who had been through battle and could protect her from anything. He worked his wetsuit up his legs and she almost gasped at the beauty of the muscles in his shoulders and arms. Finally, he pulled his wetsuit over his torso and shoulders and she found she could breathe again.

"Thanks for coming to watch me," Beck said, grinning at her as he grabbed his board.

"Sure. I love watching warriors face certain death."

He arched an eyebrow at her and she blushed. Could he read between the lines and sense her imagination in overdrive with visions of him and his bare chest?

He unlatched the trunk of his car and pulled out a beach chair. "There's a great place to watch over here and it should be good for photos."

"This is my island, remember?"

He laughed and gestured for her to walk in front. She reached for the chair, but he held onto it. "What kind of warrior would allow his lady to carry her own chair?"

"Okay, I deserved that." The awkward rhythm of her walk had color creeping up her face. Beck didn't seem to be bothered by it, but she still didn't want to be walking in front of him and having him be reminded that she wasn't perfect.

Beck set up her chair on a nice spot at the edge of the point then started picking his way down the steep hillside path to the rocks where surfers were entering the water.

"They're all nuts," Alyssa muttered. "Beck?" she called out.

He turned back and smiled at her. The sun glinted off his dark hair and his smile lit his bright blue eyes. She was lucky to be sitting down.

"Please be careful."

"Anything for you, my lady." He gave a sweeping bow and a wink.

Alyssa sent up a little prayer as he disappeared from her sight and then reappeared at the base of the hill on a huge boulder. He studied the waves crashing on the lower boulders around him, then dove into a swell that was receding from the boulders and let it carry him and his board forward for a minute. A new wave rushed toward him, but Beck simply dove under it and swam with strong strokes toward a group of surfers waiting for the ideal wave.

Other surfers picked a wave and stroked in front of it until the perfect moment when they popped up, riding proficiently. Some got tumbled pretty hard but seemed to come out of it okay. Thank heavens there were no fins visible in the water. Alyssa readied her camera quickly and snapped a lot of shots of the surfers, the ocean, and even some of the spectators around her.

She always kept one eye on Beck, gripping her camera more tightly and hoping he would be smart and safe. She had that strange sensation that someone was staring at her. She turned quickly and saw a beautiful blonde lady standing next to a sign on the hill. Alyssa gave her an uncertain smile. The lady averted her eyes and focused on the surfers. Alyssa wondered why the obviously wealthy and, in Alyssa's opinion, prissy woman would be watching her. She looked to be in her late twenties and wore a skin tight dress that definitely didn't fit with the sand, surfing, and ocean.

Alyssa turned back to watch Beck, but she was certain the blonde was looking at her again. A monstrous wave rolled toward Beck's group. He angled his board and swam quickly with the wave until the crest was almost upon him. Alyssa set her camera down, afraid she would drop it. She leaned forward, squeezing her hands tightly together, and barely able to keep from closing her eyes, like a child watching a scary movie who just wants the terrifying part to be over.

Beck jumped onto his board and skimmed along the wave. Riding into the tunnel, he twisted and turned until he reached the end and the wave petered out. He flipped into the water and then grabbed his board and started stroking back out.

Alyssa jabbed both arms into the air. "He did it!"

An older couple seated a few feet away from her laughed. She swung her gaze up the hill again. The woman gave her an imperious glare then turned and walked toward the parking lot. Alyssa smiled at the older couple and focused in on Beck again. He was too far away for her to see his features clearly, but she waved like a crazy woman at him. He lifted one hand and then went back to paddling.

The next hour Alyssa photographed Beck almost exclusively as he caught several waves, barely restraining herself from cheering each successful ride. A gigantic swell came in and she could now sense that Beck was in the right position. He paddled hard and then leapt onto his board. The tip of his board plunged forward and flipped into the roaring surge. Beck disappeared under the churning white water.

Alyssa screamed. She set her camera on the chair and stood, searching the water and praying she would see him pop out of the wave. A few seconds later he surfaced, but then the water took him down again. The wave angled toward the boulders where Beck had entered the water.

Alyssa clasped her hands to her lips. "Don't hit the rocks," she whispered.

She scurried toward the path down the incline before her mind registered what she was doing. It was ridiculous to imagine she could save him from the vicious waves or the rocks, but she couldn't sit still and watch him be pummeled. Picking her way down the rocky trail, she kept searching for Beck, hoping, praying, he'd surfaced.

He and his board flipped on top of the wave again. She caught a breath, anxious to see if he had caught one too. The wave flung him dangerously close to the boulders. Alyssa made it to the flat rock ledge and cried out his name.

Beck lay flat on his board, and without even noticing her, he started swimming back out toward the breaking waves.

"Beck!" Alyssa hollered. "Don't you dare!"

He turned at the sound of her voice. His eyes grew wide and he motioned her back.

"Don't you tell me to get back. You get out of that water before you kill yourself!"

"Alyssa!" She could hear his horrified scream over the pounding of the waves against the rocks.

Waves on the rocks? Alyssa looked up to see a wall of water hit the rock in front of her before it drove her off her feet. Her back slammed against stones and water filled her mouth and nose. The water retreated just as quickly, tugging Alyssa with it. She'd watched surfers jump into these swells and knew she'd be in serious trouble without a board to keep her afloat. She grasped for anything to stop her from being dragged into the ocean, clamping her arms around a boulder. She hung on with every ounce of strength in her arms.

The water finally receded and Alyssa found herself sprawled on the huge rock. She wanted to just stay here and rest, but the roaring in her ears told her another wave was making its way toward her. She scrambled to her feet, intent on climbing higher, but her unreliable foot slipped on the wet, mossy rocks. She went down hard and before she had time to hold her breath, water rushed over her again, pushing her toward the hillside before grabbing her in its power and trying to yank her back out to its depths. Alyssa scrambled for something solid to hang onto, but only liquid swished through her grasp. She was certain the water was going to claim her when a strong hand clasped around her arm and held tight. The water receded and she filled her lungs with salty air. Beck lifted her to her feet and ushered her toward higher ground. Alyssa shivered and clung to him as they climbed over several boulders until they were back on the trail up to the ridge.

She pushed tangled hair from her eyes and looked up into the bright blue gaze that sent warmth throughout her freezing limbs. "Oh, Beck, you're okay."

"I'm okay?" He barked a short laugh. "You almost drowned."

"I almost drowned? You were the one who almost drowned."

Beck shook his head, his eyes burning into her with a tenderness that pushed all the fear of the water taking her or anyone hurting her away. He gently lifted the hair from her cheek and then stroked his hand down the side of her face. "I was fine, sweetheart."

Alyssa's stomach fluttered at the endearment. "It scared me," she admitted, leaning closer to him.

Beck pulled her in, his strong arms chasing away any lingering fear. "I'm sorry I scared you."

"You'd better be," she muttered against the squishiness of his wetsuit.

Beck chuckled. "Is there anything I can do to make it up to you?"

She glanced up at him. "What you're doing right now seems to be working pretty well."

His grin made her wobble. He pulled her closer for a few more seconds before sighing. "We'd better get you back to Ellie. She's going to kick my rear for endangering you."

Alyssa smiled up at him. "We'll just tell her I jumped in because I couldn't stand to be away from you."

He laughed and took her hand. "She'll love that."

"Yes, she will." *Almost as much as I love being with you.* Oh, my, she was falling too hard and way too fast.

Beck wasn't thrilled with the tongue-lashing Ellie gave him, but he was certain he deserved more than that for not getting to Alyssa quicker. What had she been thinking going down to the boulders and crashing waves, to try to save him? It had felt worse than a body slam on the ice when he saw she was in danger. After he rescued her, she'd been so relieved that *he* wasn't injured. The thought made him smile. She cared about him enough to try to rescue him, even when he wasn't in any real danger.

"What are you smirking about, young man?" Ellie snapped. "My granddaughter almost drowns and you think it's funny?"

"No." Beck wiped the smile off his face and leaned forward in the wicker chair in the courtyard. Alyssa was still upstairs taking a shower. He'd rushed through his shower and went to find Granny

Ellie, knowing he had to talk to her before she got too upset. "I was smiling because..." He cleared his throat and looked down at his clasped hands. "She cares about me so much, she put herself in danger for me."

Granny thumped him on the chest. Hard. "Exactly! And if you knew what she'd been through with her weasel of a father and weak mother and all those awful men who have tried to take advantage of her." Granny tsked.

Beck's neck tightened, wanting to pry Granny for details but at the same time not wanting to know. He wished he could find some of those awful men and wallop them. He hoped with everything in him that no one had succeeded in taking advantage of his Alyssa. His Alyssa? It felt right.

"Trust is hard for her," Granny continued. "You treat her like a china doll. Got it?"

Beck met Granny's indignant blue eyes. "I promise." He meant this vow as strongly as anything he'd ever promised in his life. He would happily take care of and protect Alyssa. He was falling for her quickly and it was better than any win on the ice.

Granny straightened her thin shoulders and gave him a satisfied nod. "I've been waiting for you a long time, Beckham Taylor." She smiled. "If I croak tomorrow I'll know my Alyssa is in good hands." Granny paused and then admitted on an irritated sigh, "I'm dying, Beck."

He banged his back against the chair, shuddered out a long breath, and had to take a few moments to compose himself. He could barely resist the urge to hug the frail older woman as she looked frustrated enough to rip his head off if he showed any compassion. "Soon?" His voice cracked and he had to clear it. "I mean, not from natural causes? You aren't that old, Ellie."

"I know I look good, but I am eighty-two." She blew out a breath and shook her head. "It's the darn cancer. Took my last two husbands and now it's got me. Started with breast cancer eight years ago." She gestured to her chest and gave him a ghost of a smile. "Where do you think I got these beauties?"

Beck couldn't hold in a surprised laugh. "But you beat it."

"The first time. But I'm not willing to go through surgery and treatments again. Besides, this time it's stage four and through my entire body." She glanced up at him and shook her head as if guessing his thoughts. "Don't you give me that compassionate look and don't even think about saying sorry. I've felt fine and now the docs tell me that it won't be too long until I'm gone. All my husbands and lots of friends and family are up there waiting for me." She pointed toward the blue sky and smiled happily. She wasn't seeing Beck anymore, but a host of angels.

Beck gulped, at a complete loss for words. He'd lost his parents and brother to tragic accidents and hated the thought of death. Granny not only seemed to accept it, but be excited about it. "You're not going to do chemotherapy or radiation or, or, anything?"

"Why? No reason to be miserable when I'd rather enjoy the days I have left and then I can slip into a morphine-induced coma and wake up on the other side with all my handsome husbands waiting for me." She smiled coyly.

"But... what about Alyssa?"

Her blue eyes clouded. "That's the rub. I came here to visit her right after I found out, but I don't know how to tell her. All she'll have is Maryn and that girl isn't too reliable sometimes." She squeezed his arm. "Take care of her for me, will you?"

"What if she doesn't want me to take care of her?" Wow. Had Granny really just gone there? He was definitely enthralled with Alyssa and taking care of her sounded great, but the reality was he'd only known her a few days.

94

"She will. Give it some time and don't give up." She eyed him perceptively. "Even if things get hard. Don't give up." Granny patted his arm and smiled. "And please don't tell her we had this little chat. I'm trying to find the right time to tell her I've got to leave this old Earth, but it's going to be hard on her."

Beck nodded, unable to look away from Granny's trusting stare. A few days ago someone entrusting a beautiful woman to his care would've had him running for a fast motorcycle. Today it seemed perfectly logical, if a bit premature. Especially when a pair of long, olive-skinned legs came down the stairs with the slightly halting, but to him charming, walk that was all Alyssa. She smiled at him, her dark eyes full of promise and he knew he had finally found a woman worth caring about.

Chapter Thirteen

Beck, Alyssa, and Granny drove around the northwest side of the island early the next morning.

"The rental company told me my insurance would be void if I drove this road," Beck said, grinning.

Alyssa smiled into his twinkling blue eyes and then glanced over the sheer drop off with no guard rail on the narrow, windy strip. "Can't imagine why, I've never felt safer." She clutched the door handle and hoped Beck wouldn't notice.

"Don't worry." Beck reached across the console and took hold of her left hand. She released the door handle and relished the feel of his large hand encompassing hers. "I'll go slow."

Alyssa's breath hitched. Was he talking about driving or their relationship? She hadn't made a decision about going with him as his photographer and now her mind was a muddled mess. Was it smart to try and do a professional endeavor with a man so attractive that all she could think about was when she could get the next kiss? Beck's lips were more tempting than her chocolate stash.

"Beck!" Granny screeched.

Beck released Alyssa's hand and steered the car against the mountainside as a Jeep careened around the corner in front of them and almost plunged off the edge swerving to miss them.

Alyssa's heart thundered in her ears.

"Stop flirting and start driving," Granny commanded. "I don't mind dying, but I don't want to be mangled and live to suffer through it."

Beck gave a nervous chuckle and kept both hands on the steering wheel. They drove through gorgeous scenery, lush green mountains, and scenic drop-offs showcasing the ocean. Stopping in the quaint village of Kahakuloa, they bought a few loaves of Julia's banana bread and the villagers were great about Alyssa snapping some pictures of them. It was always a struggle to get natural pictures of people, where they weren't posing, but these people were without guile and made it easy for her.

They hiked down to the blowhole and then decided to try the Waihee Ridge Trail. Granny made it partway up the severe incline before she tottered and then sank to the ground, thumping onto her rear.

"Granny!" Alyssa cried out, bending down to steady her grandmother, amazed as always at how small she felt in her arms.

Beck hurried around and reached for Granny.

"I'm old, not a baby. These things happen to us wrinkled farts," she snapped, allowing Beck to help her to her feet then pushing him away.

Beck and Alyssa exchanged a glance over Granny's head.

"Let's go back down to the car and head to the hospital," Beck suggested.

Granny glared at him before pivoting on her heel and marching, slowly but determinedly, down toward the car. They both followed along helplessly.

"I. Am. Fine!" Granny said. "I got a little lightheaded and that is all."

There was silence as Alyssa tried to think of what to do to help Granny without offending her. Was she really okay or just trying to act tough?

They reached the car and Granny held out her hand. "Give me the keys, Beck. I'll roll down the windows and just sit here in the car, read my book, and eat banana bread. You two have fun."

"I don't want to leave you here alone," Alyssa said.

"Don't you waste your time worrying about me, I'll be perfectly happy." She shooed them with her hands. "Now go, so we can finish this crazy drive and get to Mama's Fish House in time for lunch. You owe me the market fish for making such a silly fuss over a spell of lightheadedness."

"Why don't we head there now? We'll come hike this trail another day," Beck tried.

"Do you *want* to tick me off?" Granny asked, raising her perfectly arched brows. "I didn't think so. Now you two were all excited to hike and you are going to hike. I will be fine. Got it?"

They studied each other for several charged seconds before Beck nodded slowly. "Got it." He held out his hand to Alyssa. She took it and they started up the asphalt trail. Alyssa kept sneaking glances over her shoulder at the parked car.

"We'll just go to the top of the ridge and then head back to her," Beck reassured Alyssa. "I don't want to upset her, but I also don't want to be gone too long."

"Thanks." She appreciated his concern for Granny more than she could express. "She just seems so weak lately."

Beck's jaw tightened and he squeezed her hand. "It's hard watching people you love age. My mom's parents have both passed and I miss them a lot."

They were both out of breath by the time they reached the dirt path.

"You doing okay?" Beck asked.

"I'm sweating more than my run this morning."

"We should've brought water."

"The tough hockey player shouldn't need water."

Beck winked. "You assume I'm tough. I'm really a wimp."

Alyssa glanced at his broad shoulders. "Look pretty tough to me."

He released her hand and gestured ahead of him. "Thanks. We'll have to go single file from here."

They picked their way along the path. The view of the ocean was magnificent, but as they crested the ridge line and were able to look down into the tropical valley Alyssa gasped and squeezed Beck's hand. "Look at that. Wow. It's beautiful."

She turned to see Beck staring at her instead of the scenery. "I'd say."

Alyssa blushed. Beck lifted his hand and slowly traced the line of her jaw. She trembled at his tender touch. Beck's other hand wrapped around her waist as he cupped her cheek. He studied her intently before pulling her close and lowering his face to hers. Alyssa closed her eyes and savored the warmth of his mouth. He slowly increased the intensity of the kiss. Alyssa's thoughts scattered, but she knew she'd never experienced this kind of joy and fulfillment just from being close to a man.

Voices from behind pulled them apart.

Beck smiled and clasped her hand in his. She started walking back down the trail with him close behind. The beauty of nature and the beauty of Beck. It was almost too good to be true.

A single hiker approached from below. Beck moved to the side, wrapping his arm around Alyssa's waist and directing her to the side of the trail. He smiled at her and she didn't even notice the hiker until she heard a delighted squeal of, "Beck!"

Alyssa's head whipped up. Her jaw dropped open. It was the overly-dolled-up blonde from the surfing spot yesterday. Alyssa's jaw about became unhinged when the woman threw herself into Beck's arms and planted a kiss on his lips, effectively elbowing Alyssa out of her way.

"Belle." Beck released Alyssa and placed both hands on Belle's arms. It moved the woman back a step, but Alyssa didn't like him touching her at all. "What are you doing here?"

"Vacation." She smiled like the Cheshire Cat, completely focused on Beck as if Alyssa wasn't even there. "You look fabulous, as always. How have you been?"

"Good. This is my... friend, Alyssa." Beck gave Alyssa an awkward half smile.

How Alyssa wished she could claim a better title than friend, but really, she and Beck's relationship was just too new to claim titles. Who was this woman? They seemed to be really... close. Alyssa swallowed down the jealousy that was threatening to choke her.

"Alyssa." Belle inclined her chin like she was the queen dismissing a pauper then focused back on Beck. Trailing her long, red fingernails down his chest, she smiled coyly. "I'm taking you to Roy's tonight."

Beck looked at Alyssa. "Well, um."

"Oh, yeah, *you* should go," Alyssa said, forcing a smile and scrambling for a reason to *not* tag along to Roy's with them tonight. She couldn't handle this woman looking at Beck like she owned him for ten more seconds let alone an entire dinner. If only Beck would tell Belle to get lost. *Please, please let him tell her to get lost.*

"I want you to come with us," Beck's eyes begged her to agree, but the whole situation was too awkward and she did not want to go with them tonight.

"No. You go... catch up with your friend."

Beck's face seemed to pale and Belle smiled triumphantly at Alyssa, her look saying she did not consider Beck to be just a "friend".

"Granny has been wanting to go to Miso Phat," Alyssa rushed on, speaking too quickly, "So we'll do that tonight."

Belle arched an eyebrow. "Great." She turned her fake-lashed eyes back on Beck. "I'll meet you at six."

She blew a kiss and strode up the trail, her perfect little butt swaying in such tight workout pants Alyssa could see she wasn't wearing anything underneath. Alyssa wondered what Granny would have to say about that.

Beck didn't move. Alyssa glanced at him and was surprised that his eyes were closed and he wasn't taking in the view. Thank heavens. He opened his eyes. "Sorry, that was awkward. Belle is... a good friend of my family's."

"You don't have to explain it to me," Alyssa insisted, though she wanted more than anything to know that Belle held no place in his heart.

Beck squinted at her. "Really?"

"I understand. It's no worry."

He exhaled slowly and smiled at her. "I'd much rather go to Miso Phat with you and Granny."

Alyssa shrugged. "I've heard Roy's is amazing." And the most expensive food on the island. Not that she cared.

"It's on the golf course?"

"Yeah."

"Are you into golfing?" he asked.

Alyssa knew a change of subject when she heard one. He obviously wasn't going to tell her more about the beautiful Belle and what their relationship was, but the woman had stinking kissed him on the mouth and now they were going to dinner. Alyssa's stomach turned, but she forced herself to keep a neutral expression. She'd been the one to insist that she understood.

"No. I hate it," she said. Only because her father loved it. "You?"

He shrugged and started walking slowly back down the trail. "It's fine, when I'm having a good golf day."

They didn't talk much on their way back to the car. Granny kept the conversation going throughout the interminable drive and lunch at Mama's Fish House. The food tasted like sandpaper to Alyssa.

Beck kept giving her these concerned glances, but she didn't know what to say. She couldn't stop worrying over what was going on with Granny's health and remembering Belle kissing Beck and the fact that he was meeting her for dinner tonight.

"You always a shrimp kind of guy?" Granny asked.

Beck picked up a coconut shrimp and grinned. "Pretty much. Never met a shrimp I didn't like."

Alyssa's eyes narrowed. What was he saying? He liked really thin women, like Belle, but with the addition of a fake frontal alignment. Alyssa wasn't overweight but she definitely wasn't a "shrimp" kind of girl. "Do you just like shrimpy food or shrimpy other things?" She wished she could bite her tongue, what kind of a question was that?

"Just food," Beck said.

"Hmm. Maybe you'll like *shrimp* tonight?"

"No." Beck shook his head. "Tonight I'll get steak."

"Ah, so you'll look for something more... rich tonight."

Beck cocked his head to the side and studied her, his eyebrows dipping down. Granny stared at her like she'd lost her mind.

"I need to use the restroom," Alyssa murmured. She pushed away from the table and rushed toward the back of the restaurant. Her face flamed red. Nothing like announcing that you were jealous of and concerned about the guy you liked going to dinner with a gorgeous "friend".

"What was that all about?" Granny asked Beck, stirring her Diet Coke with her straw.

Beck shook his head and shrugged. "We saw an old friend of mine on the trail. Belle asked me to go to dinner tonight and Alyssa squirmed her way out of going with us." He exhaled. Dinner would be so much better if Alyssa was there. Well, maybe, Belle could make it pretty awkward for both of them. Why was she here? Was Linli right that Belle had found out his itinerary and was now here to... what? Make life miserable for him or try to trick him into a marriage proposal? He was very much through dealing with that woman, but he really had no choice at the moment.

"Why would you agree to go to dinner with an 'old friend'?" Ellie glared at him like he and Alyssa had been married for twenty years and she'd caught him cheating.

Beck held up his hands in defense. "Honestly, I didn't want to. Belle's father donates heavily to Jordan's Buds and is on the board. It's always been like walking a tight rope trying to keep her happy so he doesn't pull out."

"Did you date her?"

"Yep." He chuckled at the anger in Granny's little body, instantly realizing that was the wrong thing to do. Her expression grew more fierce and he stifled the laughter that still wanted out. "I promise I have no feelings for her anymore, but I do have to be nice to her."

Ellie muttered something under her breath as Alyssa returned to the table with a forced smile on her face. Without Ellie contributing to the conversation and Alyssa obviously out of sorts, their day together had been pretty much toasted. For the first time since he'd met these two ladies he was happy to take them back to the bed and breakfast and say goodbye for a few hours.

Chapter Fourteen

Alyssa slipped out of her room with a basketful of laundry. Thank heavens Jerry was great to allow all of his guests to use his commercial washer and dryer. Wearing some ratty and too-short running shorts because she had no clean laundry, she padded down to the basement. She flipped the light on, but the bulbs were burned out and with only the sun coming through the doorway, it was dark and dingy in this underground room. Still, she was grateful to be able to do her laundry here rather than running to the laundromat. She leaned farther into the front-loader distributing her colored t-shirts and cotton skirts.

"I like this view," a male voice said from behind her. The door clicked closed and the room grew even dimmer, the only light now through the small window built into the door.

Alyssa whirled to cuss whoever it was out, half angry and half terrified of being alone in the semi-dark with some unknown man. The words died on her tongue when she saw the dreadlocks and the gleam in his hazel eyes. "H-How did you find me?" she asked.

The druggie from Pa'ia lifted a shoulder as his eyes roamed over her body. "There are powers in bong." He chuckled. "And sometimes I get paid well to have some fun."

He took a step forward and Alyssa tried to back away but she ran into the washer.

"Your boyfriend isn't around to protect you today."

Alyssa opened her mouth to scream. The sound might not rise

out of the small basement, but she had to try. The guy leaped across the little bit of space separating them and clasped his hand over her mouth. "If you scream I'll make this much worse on you."

Alyssa nodded against his hand, pretending she would cooperate while she scrambled for any idea to escape.

He smirked. "Don't think I'm stupid, little girl. I can see in your eyes that you like to fight."

She sunk her teeth into the disgusting flesh of his hand. He howled and yanked it away. Alyssa screamed for all she was worth and jabbed her fist into his gut. He leaned forward and she felt a surge of pride. That was a strong punch. Stomping on his foot, she pushed around him and scurried toward the door.

His hand wrapped around her arm, jerking her to a halt.

"Help, please help!" Alyssa hollered at the top of her lungs. She clawed at his hand with her fingernails.

"You little wench," he panted. "I am not getting paid enough to put up with this."

The door burst open behind her. Beck's wide shoulders blocked out the sun, but the scowl on his face was easily readable.

The guy released Alyssa and she fell. Beck caught her, holding her against his side with one strong arm. The guy was the one backing up now.

"Hey. I wasn't going to hurt her," he said, holding up both palms.

Beck ushered Alyssa behind him and advanced on the guy. Alyssa was glad he was on her side. "You'll regret even looking at her," Beck said.

"No, it isn't like that. Some stiff paid me to scare her."

"Who paid you?" he growled.

"I don't know. Some old guy in a sweet Lexus."

A Lexus. Alyssa covered her mouth with her hand. No. It couldn't be. She thought she'd seen someone who looked like her dad the first time this guy attacked her. Did her dad follow her to Hawaii? He hadn't protected her when she'd been attacked by Hugh, but would he really stoop so low as to pay someone to hurt her? Everything was about financial gain with her father. The question was, if he was involved, how could this help him make a profit? It didn't make sense.

Beck withdrew his phone from his pocket and handed it to Alyssa. "Call the police."

The guy jumped and tried to scurry around them. Beck grabbed the front of his shirt and slammed him against the wall like they were in a hockey game. "Don't move," he demanded.

Alyssa quickly dialed 911 and after a short conversation was reassured that officers would be there momentarily. Moments seemed to drag as the guy squirmed, swore, begged, and threatened while Beck held him in place. The police finally came and took their statements then hauled the guy away. She didn't mention her father to anyone and prayed it was all an awful coincidence.

Finally it was just her and Beck. He gently escorted her to the courtyard. Two fat tears rolled down her cheeks. She'd felt numb as the police had questioned her, but now the fear was all rushing back. Beck wrapped her up in his arms and simply held her.

"You did great," he murmured against her hair. "You're safe now. I've got you."

Alyssa melted against him, so grateful he was here, that he'd come for her. She shut out the fact he was going to dinner with Belle tonight. For this moment, it was enough to just be in his arms.

Chapter Fifteen

Beck met Belle at Roy's, the exclusive restaurant on the Ka'anapali Golf Course. He wished she'd worn taller heels so he couldn't see straight down her cleavage line, but maybe they didn't make heels taller than four inches. She reached up to kiss him the moment he walked in, but he turned his head so she only brushed his cheek. He was not having a repeat of her pressing her hard lips to his like she had this morning.

He kept his practiced smile on and prayed he could get through the night without offending her and losing her dad, Joseph's, support. Joseph was a good guy overall and had been on the board of Jordan's Buds since its conception. The money he donated made a difference to thousands of children. When Beck had refused to give into both of their father's wishes and ask Belle to marry him five years ago, he was afraid he'd lost her dad too. Joseph had surprised him. He'd assured Beck as long as he was respectful to his girl he would still support him and Jordan's Buds.

Beck hid a sigh as Belle prattled on about some trip to Greece. The woman spent more money on shopping in exotic locations than most countries did on defense. He just had to get through dinner and then he could hopefully find Alyssa. Things had been awkward at lunch today, but after he protected her from that idiot she'd all but melted in his arms.

He hated to leave her tonight after what she'd been through this afternoon. She kept insisting she would be fine, but he had a hard time believing her. He couldn't imagine the terror she must be feeling, being attacked by that same guy and finding out someone had paid him to do it. Maybe Beck could take her out for dessert to bring her smile back. His smile at Belle actually became real as he thought about Alyssa and how she tasted better than any dessert he could recall. He wondered what Granny Ellie would do if he called her granddaughter dessert. He almost laughed then. Ellie would probably tell him to savor it.

"Park right there," Granny screeched.

Alyssa stared at the red paint on the curb. "That's not a spot. They'll tow my car."

"I'll pay if you get a ticket. Now park."

Alyssa shook her head, but obeyed. There was no use arguing when Granny was in a mood.

"If we don't hurry, we're going to miss him."

Granny sprung from the car and took off across the golf course. Alyssa looked around, hoping they wouldn't get beaned in the head with a golf ball. This was nuts. She followed Granny across two open green spaces and though they didn't get hit or stopped, they did get some strange looks.

Granny tugged on Alyssa's hand as they rounded a putting green and saw the restaurant a hundred yards away.

"We're going to get kicked out of here," Alyssa muttered. She had no idea how she'd allowed Granny to talk her into spying on Beck and Belle. She had no desire to see them together. Talk about the stuff of nightmares. Sadly, she never told Granny no.

"You shush. We'll be fine. I've been a spy so many times someone should pay me."

Alyssa laughed, glancing over at her Granny decked out in a black hat, long-sleeved shirt, and pants. Luckily she'd decided the black face paint was a pain, sharing lengthy stories of several excursions with her best friend Ruby where the paint had flaked off.

It wasn't quite dark yet, but at least most of the golfers were gone. Tiki torches lit the patio of Roy's Restaurant. Alyssa and Granny covered the last fifty yards and Alyssa immediately picked out Beck. She swallowed. He looked fabulous in a short-sleeved button-down shirt, open at the collar. He smiled at Belle. It looked practiced at first then it became genuine and Alyssa felt like she'd been punched in the gut. He obviously liked Belle to share a smile like that with her.

She tried not to look at Belle, but it was impossible not to notice the low-cut and ultra-short red dress. Belle crossed her legs and Alyssa wondered if the woman knew what underwear was. This was the second time she'd seen Belle and she was pretty sure she'd seen more of her than she ever wanted to see of another woman.

"Holy crap, what a hooker," Granny said.

"Shh." Alyssa pulled her behind a huge banyan tree. "We've seen them, now let's get out of here."

Granny peeked around to take a look at the couple once more. "Just a minute. We've worked too hard to find out what's going on here. I'm not leaving until I have some reassurance that my boy is just being a gentleman with an old friend." She studied the couple as Alyssa picked at a hangnail and focused on the setting sun over the ocean. This was a beautiful view. If only she could enjoy it.

"Oh," Granny said. "Oh, my. Oh, no."

Alyssa couldn't stand it. She peeked around the tree and saw Belle's full chest pressed against Beck's arm as he held the menu and ordered his food. Alyssa glanced down at her much smaller bosom and knew she couldn't compete physically with a surgically constructed woman like Belle. Turning back to the ocean, she took long, slow inhalations.

"You have got to be kidding me," Granny muttered. "Be strong, Beck."

Alyssa wished she could be strong too, but of course she glanced again. Belle dropped her napkin and leaned all the way over to pick it up. Alyssa was certain the girl did not hold stock in Victoria's Secret. I mean, come on. A bra would at least rein those puppies in. She couldn't bring herself to look at Beck and see the admiration or lust or whatever men had on their faces at such a moment.

Granny blew out a breath and said, "Well, this spy mission sucked." She turned to Alyssa. Her blue eyes soft with sympathy. "Forget Miso Phat. Ice cream for dinner?"

Alyssa forced a smile. "Maybe that would help."

Granny wrapped an arm around Alyssa's waist and they trudged back the way they'd come. It was sad when even Granny realized there was no purpose in spying any more. Belle was gorgeous and Beck was obviously having a great time, touching, looking at, and whatever else he was going to do with her. Alyssa hated herself for falling for Beck so quickly. He'd seemed so different, but apparently was ruled by lust like every other guy she'd dated.

"I should've known," she muttered.

"What was that?" Granny asked over her shoulder.

"Men suck," Alyssa said louder.

Granny fell into step with Alyssa and wrapped an arm around her waist. "They do sometimes, but I can't help loving them for their bodies."

Alyssa laughed uneasily, but didn't agree. Belle could keep Beck's gorgeous body. Alyssa was done competing. Sadness ripped through her. She'd given Beck up voluntarily. Why did it have to hurt so much?

Chapter Sixteen

The next morning Alyssa ran some trails above the bed and breakfast. She didn't usually run alone on trails, but she had her can of pepper spray and she was having a really hard time caring about much of anything today. She was miserable. All she could picture was how gorgeous Belle had looked at dinner in her tight, low-cut dress and how Beck had seemed completely focused on her. Would Alyssa hear from him again? If she did, what would she say? *I'm not mature enough to travel with you and help the children unless you promise to only look at me in that special way?* Aarggh. She thought she'd written men off and now she was a jealous mess over the first one she fell for.

Her foot throbbed. Uneven paths tended to do that, but she forced herself to keep pounding out the steps. Eventually, the physical exertion would become all-consuming and she'd forget the ache in her foot and the ache over losing Beck. At least that was the theory.

Footsteps thudded from behind and Alyssa picked up her pace. She didn't like seeing other runners when she was in an isolated spot. Paranoia was protection sometimes. But the runner kept coming and coming and then she heard her name, "Alyssa! Please... wait."

Alyssa turned as Beck sprinted up to her. She wasn't sure if she was relieved it was him or not.

"Hey," he gasped out, resting his hands on his thighs.

"Hey." She glanced over the well-defined muscles of his upper body, too evident in the tight neoprene shirt he wore. She forced herself not to remember how good it felt to be cuddled into that chest and folded her arms across her midsection.

111

"You didn't answer my texts," he said, straightening up and wiping away the sweat on his forehead.

"I don't bring my phone when I run." She was such a liar. Her phone was tucked in her shorts pocket.

"I texted you last night about going for ice cream or something."

"Oh, those texts." She pressed her lips together. "I wasn't up for a threesome."

"Not with Granny. Just you and me."

"I wasn't talking about Granny."

He cocked his head to the side and studied her. Alyssa sighed when it became apparent he wasn't going to make this easy on her. She closed her eyes and muttered, "Belle."

Beck's eyebrows arched up. "What about her?"

Her stomach clenched. His inflection hadn't been harsh, but sadly it had sounded exactly like the many times her mom had found out about another woman and her dad had sweet-talked her out of believing he'd cheated. That was years ago though, when her dad used to keep up the pretense of being faithful.

"I'm not into two-timers, Beck." She turned and ran away, unfortunately the trail was a steep incline and she was panting within seconds.

Beck caught her easily and wrapped her in his arms, hauling her to a stop. Alyssa's breath was coming in sharp bursts, from the run, her anger, the feel of his touch, or the embarrassment over her petty behavior, she wasn't sure. She elbowed him in the gut. He grunted and released her. Alyssa whirled to face him.

Beck held his hands up. "Hey, it's okay," he soothed.

Alyssa eyed him warily.

"I would never two-time you, Alyssa."

"I wish I could believe that."

His dark hair glistened in the sunlight and his blue eyes were sparking. "I'm confused, Alyssa. You said you understood about me going to dinner with Belle."

She groaned. She had said that, but she hadn't meant it. "I thought I did, but... it seems like it was more than dinner."

"It wasn't." Beck took a cautious step forward. "Belle is a good friend of my family's. We got together last night to catch up, nothing more. Her dad contributes heavily to my charities and has been like an uncle to me."

Alyssa swallowed and nodded bravely. "That's all?"

"That's all." He cupped her face with his hands and Alyssa was very proud of herself for not melting into a puddle at his feet. He traced his thumb down her cheek and she trembled.

"Did you ever date her?" She hated herself for asking, but she needed to know.

"Yes." He released her face.

"How serious?"

He exhaled and shook his head. "It's been years since we dated and it doesn't matter anymore."

Alyssa felt like it very much did matter. She hated that Beck was closing the subject and she didn't know how to keep it open without sounding like an insecure wimp. This entire conversation was too reminiscent of her dad and his dismissal of all of her mom's fears. Her mom had been the stupid sap that had always fallen back into his traps.

"You're right," Alyssa muttered. "It doesn't matter. You're just like my father. Apparently all men are." Oh, no. Had she really just said that? It was too late to take it back now and in her irrational jealous anger she didn't want to. She caught a glimpse of Beck's face before she brushed past him and raced up the trail. He looked shocked and angered by her barbed words. It really was unfair to compare him to her father. Alyssa regretted the insult but no way was she going to retrace her steps and chat it all out with him.

After a while Alyssa realized there were no footsteps following her. He'd given up on her. Tears raced down her cheeks. Beck not following her shouldn't hurt this bad, but she realized that she wanted more than anything for him to convince her that he was different, that he did care. Her mind replayed every word he'd said and every picture of him and Belle together as she pounded through the miles.

When she finally returned home to shower, the worries of Belle and the memories of her dad's infidelity were so strong she could hardly catch a full breath. Beck had seemed so genuine, but it was just like always... she couldn't allow herself to trust a man.

Chapter Seventeen

Beck was barely out of the shower when he heard a firm knock on his door. He swung it wide, hoping for Alyssa, even though her parting line had ticked him off so much he didn't know when or if they were going to make up. She and Ellie had all but called her father a sleaze then Alyssa said she was just like him. That hurt.

A man stood on the landing with white-blond hair and blue eyes regarding him with a calculating stare.

"Can I help you?" Beck asked.

"I certainly think you can." The man extended his hand and smiled. "Gary Armsworth. I think we have a mutual concern."

Beck shook the man's soft hand as an automatic response, in shock Alyssa's dad would track him down. "Concern?"

"My sweet Alyssa." Gary walked past Beck before he could protest. Beck softly shut the door behind him. How dare Alyssa trounce on his heart and then send her dad to what... chat with him?

"My sources tell me that you've taken advantage of my daughter."

"What?" Beck's neck muscles tightened. Alyssa wouldn't have told him that, would she? Possibly Ellie. But both of them acted like they didn't trust or like this guy. Beck could see why already. He made Beck feel like he needed another shower. "What sources? I haven't done anything but kiss her."

Gary arched an eyebrow. "You want more than a simple kiss and you love her."

Beck swallowed. Yesterday he might have reluctantly agreed with either statement. After this morning, he was too upset to know what to think. Alyssa had seemed like his dream girl and then she'd accused him of checking out Belle and being a scumbag like the weasel standing in front of him.

"I'm willing to grant you permission to have fun with her, or even marry her if that's more your style." He grinned and spread his hands wide.

Beck thought punching this guy in the face might be more his style. Who offered up their own daughter to an unknown man to "have fun with"?

"I have a business proposition for you," Gary continued. "Might as well keep the business in the family, right?" He nudged Beck's arm.

Beck had no clue how to respond. "Business proposition?" He remembered Alyssa's response to those words. No wonder she had been so skittish with a father who acted like this. He wondered if he felt more pity for Alyssa having to deal with this guy or more anger that she'd compared Beck to him.

"I understand you manage extensive real estate holdings. I happen to be in real estate too; I own several title agencies. So here's my proposition: you use one of my title companies for all of your transactions," He extended a business card, "and I'll encourage Alyssa to choose you. Help you have all the fun with my daughter you desire."

Beck didn't take the card. He didn't like this guy, at all, and the way he'd said, "have fun with my daughter" had Beck itching to plant a fist in his face. How many other men had received a similar offer and taken advantage of it. Had Alyssa given in to any of them? A sour taste filled his mouth. "And if I *can't* use your title companies for some of my transactions?"

"We're throughout the west, it won't be a problem."

"I think it might be. I'm happy with my current business

relationships." Beck arched an eyebrow, daring the guy to contradict him. Gary had done his homework. Between Jordan's Buds and all of Beck's family's real estate holdings he used title companies a lot and this would be a significant boost to any title company.

The man's blue eyes, that looked an awful lot like Ellie's, narrowed and cooled to ice. "I think you'll want to switch." He set the card on a side table. "I can make a lot of trouble for you and Alyssa. I don't think you want that." He opened the door.

"No one threatens me," Beck muttered. He grabbed the card and flicked it at Gary. It fell to the floor and neither man moved to pick it up. Beck took a step forward. "If you ever try to extort me again, I will press charges." He was struggling through the anger of Alyssa comparing him to this jerk and his compassion at her being raised by such a loser. Despite her final comment this morning, he cared for her more than he wanted to believe. "Threaten Alyssa again and we'll see who can make trouble for who."

Gary sneered at him. "Hawaii is a dangerous place. I'd hate for someone else to attack my precious daughter. There's no saying what kind of diseases the druggies around here are carrying."

Beck's eyes widened. "Are you driving a silver Lexus sport utility?"

Gary backed out onto the balcony. "I don't see that what I drive matters to you."

"You paid that idiot to hurt Alyssa," Beck growled. "What kind of a father are you?"

"I don't know what you're talking about." Gary turned and walked a few steps away.

Beck followed him. "You try to hurt Alyssa again and I'll think about turning you into the police, if there's enough of you left after I pummel you." Beck couldn't believe how overprotective he felt of Alyssa. She didn't deserve a father like this and he was having a hard time blaming her for being distrusting after being around Gary for five minutes.

Gary didn't respond, taking the stairs two at a time.

Beck debated going after him, but he felt like having leverage on a man like that was the better course. After the way Gary took off out of there, Beck was pretty sure they wouldn't hear from him again.

He stalked back into his room and sunk onto the bed, sick that Alyssa and Ellie had to deal with that man. His father would've never treated people like cattle. Beck didn't know what to think about Alyssa now. He wanted to talk with her, look into her dark eyes, and see if they had a chance. Had her comment about him being like her father been said out of hurt because she thought Beck cared for Belle? Maybe. He'd never know if he didn't get brave enough to ask. He looked at his clenched fists. He was brave enough to fight anyone on the ice or off, but was he brave enough to use those same fists to pound on the door of the woman he thought he'd fallen for? He unclenched his fingers and sighed. Not sure of his answer.

Chapter Eighteen

Alyssa had taken her time showering and sorting through some photos. Luckily Granny slept late each morning so she had a few minutes to dry her tears and try to figure out how to break the news to Granny. She'd offended Beck with her comment about him being like her father and she probably wouldn't see him again. A despair so heavy it seemed to choke her spread throughout her body. Sadly, the next picture was one of Beck kicking a ball around with some children from the village where they bought banana bread yesterday.

She traced the lines of his face and whispered, "Oh, Beck." Had she been wrong about him? She sure thought he was different, before Belle had shown up.

A hard rap on her door almost made her drop her laptop. "Coming," she called.

She wiped at her face and tried to force a smile as she cracked the door open. Beck stood on the other side. His eyes stormy like rough seas. His face softened visibly when he saw her and his massive shoulders, that had been bunched around his ears, lowered.

Alyssa pulled the door open wider. "Beck," she breathed.

"Hey." He pushed a hand through his dark hair. "Can we talk?"

She nodded and backed away from the door.

Beck entered, filling up the small room.

"I'm sorry," she muttered before he could say anything.

He swallowed and said, "Sorry for what?"

"I shouldn't have compared you to my father." She hung her head, unable to meet his gaze.

Beck gently tilted her chin up with his fingers. Alyssa's breath caught. He was so close she could smell the clean, crisp scent of his body. Her eyes flickered from the breadth of his chest to meet his gaze. His blue eyes were finally warm. They finally looked like her Beck.

"Thank you." He released her face but didn't step back. "But I think it's me that needs to apologize. I didn't realize... how uncertain you were of men."

"You mean terrified?" she bit her lip, not sure why she'd let that escape. No one but Maryn knew how scared she was.

"Is that a better way to describe it?"

"Maybe." She played with the bottom of her shirt.

"It all hit me when... well, a little bit ago. You didn't spend any time alone with me before you got to know me. You seemed almost scared of me and it didn't make sense." He captured her hand and stroked his thumb along the back of it. "Can you tell me about it?"

Alyssa's breath caught as she met his gaze. "My father used to let his friends play around me with. They never went too far, but... Oh, man." It was so hard to explain this. "They would tease me and make me sit on their laps. They just made me feel gross and made me think that all men were takers." She shook her head, not sure how much she wanted to spell out to him as his grip on her hand tightened. "Then I found a boyfriend in college that I thought was great. We went away for spring break and he came through the adjoining door and tried to make me... well, you know." The grip got tighter. "Ouch." Alyssa tugged her fingers back.

"Sorry." Beck released her hand and jammed his fingers through his already mussed dark hair. "There's more, isn't there?"

"You don't want to hear it all."

Beck's eyes were full of compassion. "I can handle whatever you want to tell me."

Alyssa licked her lips and admitted, "I dated a politician after college. He fulfilled the stereotypes, telling everybody, including me, whatever we wanted to hear. He cheated on me." She found as she got going it was hard to stop. "I have nightmares every few weeks about a man who tried to rape me." She hung her head. "My father was going to sell me to him."

Beck gave a strangled groan and backed into the door. "Oh, Alyssa."

She shook her head. "I'm a mess, Beck. Maybe you don't want to deal with my insecurities."

"Alyssa," he breathed her name. "I can deal with a lot if I can be with you."

Alyssa focused on his blue eyes. There was so much truth in them. Would he really be there for her, even when she got scared and wanted to run? "You can?" her voice pitched up too high and she cleared her throat.

"Yes." He raised his hands like he wanted to touch her, but wasn't sure if she would welcome it. "So, where do we go from here?""

She wanted to yank his head down and kiss the daylights out of him, but she had to ask. "Um, can you tell me about you and Belle?

"Please don't worry about Belle," he said. "I'd much rather be with you."

"You would?"

"I'll prove it to you. I would never do this to Belle." He crossed the small distance between them and wrapped his arms around her back. "Is this okay?"

Alyssa nodded. "I love when you touch me."

He grinned then lowered his head and gently caressed her lips with his. Alyssa couldn't hold in a sigh from the sweetness of his touch.

"Beck," she whispered. She shook her head to clear it and pulled free of his arms. Shame filled her. She was a distrusting brat, but she wanted him to know. "We followed you last night and spied on you and Belle. Granny forced me."

Beck chuckled. "Only Granny."

"You aren't mad?" Her dad would've been furious if her mom would've done something like that. Then he would've calmed down and talked her back into loving him.

"No, because that gives me the proof I need."

"What do you mean?"

"Did you see me do anything with Belle?"

Alyssa paused and thought. "Well, you smiled at her."

Beck grinned. "Was it anything like the smile I'm giving you right now?" Again he was in her space and she was having a hard time breathing.

"I guess not. It was more... practiced."

"Exactly."

"And she was cuddled against you."

"What?" His eyebrows almost met his hairline.

"When you ordered."

"Oh, no. That's not fair. She pressed against me, but I moved as soon as I could."

Hmm. She could believe that. "And you checked her out when she dropped something."

"Whoa." He held up his hands. "I absolutely did not check her out. I was checking my phone and hoping you were texting me." He grinned. "Oh, and I was looking at the pictures I snapped of us when we were snorkeling with Captain Aaron."

"What? I looked horrible in those."

"You always look beautiful."

"You didn't check her out?"

"I promise I didn't. Did it look like I was?"

"Actually, I didn't look at you. I was too busy noticing everything she was displaying."

Beck grimaced. "She has a horrible habit of showing off too much."

"Every man likes that."

"That's not fair. Come on, Lyssa."

She warmed clear through at his tender use of the nickname Stockton had given her.

"I'm not some scumbag who just wants to check out a woman in tight, revealing clothing. If you want to see my face when I check a woman out I'll show you." He held out her arms and rested his hands on her hips. He turned her to one side and then the other. His eyebrows lifted, he grinned, and his eyes roamed over her. "Now that is a shape worth checking out."

Alyssa didn't want to, but laughter bubbled out of her. She knew she couldn't compare with a team of plastic surgeons shaping the perfect body, but she loved the admiration in Beck's eyes. "You're trying to convince me you don't want to be with her?"

He wrapped his arms around her. "I made it through dinner, but it wasn't fun. I realized when I got back to the bed and breakfast that I hadn't smiled or laughed for real all night. I should've gone to your room and begged you to go for ice cream. I wanted to smile with you, Lyssa. I assumed when you didn't answer my texts you were already in bed."

"So you didn't give her real smiles?" Alyssa shook her head at how silly this was. She was jealous of Beck giving out his smiles?

"I don't give real smiles to anyone but you." Beck slowly lowered his head to hers, stopping a breath away from her mouth. "Except for my nieces and nephews."

"Okay, I'll make allowances for them." She wanted him to cross those centimeters separating them.

Beck smiled against her mouth and whispered, "And I'm not doing this with anyone but you." He kissed her with just the right amount of pressure, wrapping his strong arms around her back and pulling her in full contact with his body. Alyssa moaned in delight and matched the passion in his kiss with her own fire. She'd never been so consumed by someone's touch. Beck continued to work his magic on her mouth and her body molded itself to his.

Much, much later, Beck and Alyssa found Granny and took her to dinner at the Mixed Plate. Beck actually spit some water across the table, laughing at Granny asking the sweet Chinese lady if her chicken was real or was actually dog meat. The language barrier didn't stop the woman from being severely offended, but Granny had remained convinced it was actually dog. "Chicken isn't stringy like this," she muttered.

Granny begged off walking on the beach after dinner, saying she needed to rest. The mischievous twinkle in her eye wasn't missed by either of them when they dropped her off at the bed and breakfast.

They walked along Ka'anapali and watched for whale spouts as the sun set.

"Tell me about the rest of your family," Beck asked.

Alyssa shrugged, squishing sand between her toes with each step. She didn't even feel unsteady with her foot, not with Beck's arm around her waist. "Not much to tell. Just my mom. No siblings that I know of."

"That you know of?"

She took a long breath before admitting, "My dad's a piece of work. He never married my mom, but insisted I take his name. The only good thing he gave me, besides financial support, is Granny Ellie."

"She's great." Beck grinned at her and Alyssa wondered if the sand shifted or if her blood sugar might be low. She swayed and his arm tightened around her waist. "You feeling okay?"

"Better now." She smiled stupidly at him.

Beck pulled her closer and they continued their stroll. "Where are your parents now?"

"Mom's current house is in Pelican Shores."

"Oh." The lifted eyebrows said he knew exactly how much it cost to live in the exclusive southern California neighborhood. "And your dad?" His voice was cold like he already didn't like her dad. She thought he must be a good judge of character.

"Who knows? He floats through houses and women and he travels a lot." She swallowed. "My mom is a very beautiful lady, relocated from the Philippines when she was a teenager. She was so poor as to be starving at times. Dad found her and offered her security and…" It was so embarrassing to admit this to him. "Granny claims my mom is co-dependent. It's messed up. Granny taught me to be strong and never rely on a man for anything." She smiled. "I used to think Granny Ellie was a hypocrite marrying all the wealthy men she did, but then I realized that she really loved each of her husbands and she had her own career too, 'Top realtor in Franklin County'." She grinned, thinking of all the times Granny had bragged about that and how few realtors there actually were in Franklin County, Idaho.

"Pretty cool lady."

"Thanks. I'd be lost without her." She studied the waves and tried to shift the focus of the conversation. "What about you, any siblings?"

"Two sisters. They're both older and happily married."

"Nieces or nephews?"

"Anna has three boys. They're wild little monkeys and just crack me up. Shelby adopted two girls from China. They're really cute and give the best hugs, but they're kind of prissy. It's funny to watch them react to Anna's boys."

She smiled wistfully. "I want a whole houseful of boys to wrestle with."

"Really? No girls for you?"

"Not sure I could relate to playing Barbie's and princesses, but I'm sure a girl would be a lot of fun too." She looked up at him and blushed. "What?"

"Nothing. I just like what I learn about you."

They walked in silence for a few minutes then Alyssa dared to ask, "Do your brothers-in-law help you run your business?"

"Anna's husband, Peter, is a real estate attorney. He's great to offer pro bono work for Jordan's Buds. Shelby's husband, Ross, is a plastic surgeon, so he travels with me quite often to provide medical care to the orphanages. He's done over a hundred cleft palette repairs. Both of my sisters married well. Dad insisted upon that."

"Are they happy?"

"Ecstatically."

"That's what's important." She looked askance at him. "Did your dad have someone in mind for you to marry well too?"

His eyes darkened. "Yeah, but he died too soon to force me into it."

"How did they die?" She couldn't believe she'd just asked that, especially since she knew from the article Maryn had done years ago. When he found out she knew so much about him and had taken paparazzi pictures, he was going to think she was a liar. She didn't know how to bring that subject up, but she needed to do it soon. Beck was supposed to be leaving the island in just a couple of days. She also wondered who his dad had been planning on him marrying. Belle? That was a horrible thought. "You don't have to tell me about it if you don't want."

"It's okay. I'm doing a lot better with it. Dad loved showing off his money almost more than I like hiding the fact that I have money. Fast motorcycles were his thing. They were on a Dodge Tomahawk racing along Highway One, close to Big Sur."

She sucked in a breath.

"You know that spot?"

"Yeah. It's so pretty, but scary to drive."

"They were driving way too fast. Went off an edge and..."

The beautiful sunset was lost on Beck as he studied their feet.

"Have you forgiven him?"

"Hard to blame him when I understand." He sighed and clenched his fist.

Alyssa tilted his chin up. "You... understand?"

His eyes filled with sadness.

"Can you tell me about it?"

Beck tugged her toward a privacy wall for one of the resorts. They sank down into the sand and rested their backs against the wall.

"My scars aren't all from hockey and I don't just have two sisters." He took a long breath and released it. "I had a little brother, Jordan." He half-smiled. "Loved that kid. He idolized me and we had the best time together. When I was a senior in high school he was eight. We both loved dad's motorcycles and I'd take him on rides all the time. One day we were on Laguna Canyon Road. I was going too fast and I hit some gravel. We took out a guardrail, went down hard..." Tears squeezed out of his eyelids and he didn't finish.

Alyssa wrapped both her arms around his strong shoulders and held him close. He buried his head in her chest and it about ripped Alyssa's heart out when he stifled a sob. Alyssa knew as he clung to her that she would do anything for this man. Tomorrow she'd find the right time to tell him about the pictures and Maryn. This definitely wasn't that moment, but right now she could tell him she'd made a decision. She'd go with him and they'd start a new life together. She'd capture the children's suffering and their happiness and together they would change lives because she'd be with Beck.

"Beck," she whispered.

He lifted his head and cleared his throat. "Wow. Sorry." He managed a smile then leaned in and kissed her. Alyssa forgot everything she wanted to say as she savored his touch and the passion in his kiss. He broke away and trailed his hands through her hair.

"I'll go with you," she said.

He arched an eyebrow.

"I'll be your photographer. Let's travel the world and save some cute kiddos."

Beck laughed and shook his head. "Let's do it. But first..." He tilted her chin up and proceeded to take advantage of her mouth for several wonderful minutes. When he stopped they were both breathing hard. "Can that be part of the arrangement?" Beck asked.

"I wouldn't go without it." Alyssa grinned and kissed him again.

Chapter Nineteen

"Good morning, Beckham. It's Gary, Alyssa's father."

Beck froze. His hand gripped his phone tightly. How had he gotten this number? Linli's paranoia seemed to be warranted, for once. "What do *you* want?"

"I want you to take care of my little girl." He gave a nasty chuckle. "And since you wouldn't agree to using my title companies, I'll settle for five million dollars."

Beck laughed shortly. "Just stay away from Alyssa and I won't have to come find you."

"Look under the door, Beckham."

Beck strode to the door and picked up a glossy magazine that had been slid under. The front page had a picture of him and Alyssa strolling arm in arm down Ka'anapali Beach. "What is this?" he growled.

"Read the article, Beckham. Then you'll realize what I'm capable of and there's much more where that came from if you don't think you can afford my fee for staying away. I'd also like your reassurance that my Alyssa is going to be very, very happy. I'm sure you don't want your sisters or nieces and nephews exposed. I'll be in touch with wire transfer instructions. If I don't see the money by tomorrow at this time, another story about Alyssa selling herself to my friends and you murdering your little brother will go live. This one is pretty complimentary in comparison."

The line went dead before Beckham could tell Alyssa's dad

exactly what he thought about his threats. He'd happily take care of Alyssa, but where did the guy get off trying to blackmail him? He ripped the magazine open.

Alyssa felt her world light up as Beck strode to the table where she was enjoying her breakfast of papaya and cottage cheese in the bright morning sun. The light started to dim when she saw the raw hurt and anger in his eyes.

"Beck?" She stood. "Wh-what happened?"

He slammed a magazine onto the table, glowering at her. "You happened."

"What?"

The front cover was a picture of the two of them walking on the beach with his arm wrapped around her. "Billionaire ex-NHL star Beckham Taylor falls in love with the photographer who stalked him."

"But you can't think I..."

"Read the article and then try to tell me what I think." He shook his head. "And to think I trusted you. You can't blackmail me, Alyssa. You're worse than the women who I *knew* were just after my money. What a scheme, eh?" He cocked an eyebrow at her. "Ellie, your dad, the druggie. How long did it take you to plan it all?"

"What? I didn't—" Her dad? What did her dad have to do with any of this?

"It just kills me that you and Granny Ellie could do it." His blue eyes lit up with fire. "She's not really dying, is she? That was all part of your scheme too!"

"Granny, dying?" Alyssa sank into the chair, terror ripping through her. It wasn't true. It couldn't be.

"Don't act so innocent, Alyssa, I'm done believing the act."

Anger seared into her as pieces started snapping into place. Granny was really dying. Beck knew and he hadn't even told her. Who cared about some article Maryn had included them in? "Granny told you she was dying and you didn't *tell* me?" She leapt to her feet and hurried around the table, coming up into his face.

"Well, it doesn't seem to matter now as it was all an act," Beck snarled.

"Granny would never lie to you!" Alyssa shrieked. Her entire body trembled. She didn't know which fear to tackle first, losing Granny or losing Beck, so she held onto her anger.

"But you would?" Beck's voice lowered and quivered slightly.

"No!" She backed away as she realized she hadn't told him the entire truth. Maryn and the pictures came to mind. What did this article say?

Beck jerked the magazine into his hand, opened it to a page filled with pictures of the two of them and slapped it back down on the table. "I can't believe anything you say anymore, Alyssa. Read that and try to lie to me again." He whirled and stormed across the courtyard.

Alyssa started reading, unable to comprehend what Maryn had done to her, to him. Tears leaked out of her eyes and rolled down her face. Almost a dozen pictures of her and Beck together. Someone must've been stalking them, but they claimed Alyssa had been stalking him for years, starting with taking photographs of him and his sister after the funeral. The article claimed Alyssa had a fatalistic kind of crush on him and was trying to fulfill the Billionaire Bride Pact she'd made as a twelve-year old by snaring Beck. They claimed she needed money because she'd rejected her, oh so concerned parents. What a crock. Some truth was there, but of course they'd twisted it and made her look like a black widow spider stalking her prey. Maryn was listed as the writer.

Alyssa groaned and buried her head on the table. "Oh, Maryn."

Then the thought of Granny dying slammed into her gut. It couldn't be true. She'd lost Beck. She couldn't survive without Granny.

Chapter Twenty

Luckily it was his brother-in-law, Peter, who picked Beck up at the airport. Beck had chartered the fastest jet he could find and was home within hours of his fight with Alyssa. He fought his way through the paparazzi, ignoring questions about his relationship with Alyssa. Someone called her a gold-digging tramp and it was all Beck could do to not punch the reporter. How could he honestly want to break down and run back to Maui every time he heard her name?

Peter swung open the door of his Maserati. "Let's go."

Beck slid in gratefully. "Thanks for coming. I couldn't handle one of my sisters right now." He loved them, but being the younger brother of overprotective women got old, quick.

"I know, man. I know. Don't worry about Mr. Armsworth printing any more articles. We've already bought the majority shares of the magazine, informed the editors what will happen if they print any more articles about you, and we would've fired the writer, a Maryn Howe, but she'd already quit. We'll devalue the stocks and make sure Mr. Armsworth loses a lot of money before we run him out then we'll go after Miss Armsworth."

"Not Miss Armsworth."

"What? She played you like a saxophone."

Beck swallowed and looked out the window.

"No. You fell for her. Hard."

Beck could only nod.

"I'm sorry."

"Me, too." He thought of the way Alyssa had looked as he'd sneaked around the back entrance of the bed and breakfast and seen her with her head down in the magazine, tears wetting the pages. She'd sent him multiple texts apologizing, professing her innocence, claiming that a friend of hers and the magazine were to blame and that she could explain about the pictures of him and his sister. Could any of it be true? His stomach clenched. No. He'd been fooled by beautiful women before. But he'd never fallen in love with any of them.

Chapter Twenty-one

Alyssa thought she'd cried all her tears when Granny banged on the door to her room, hugged her, and demanded she tell her what happened, but the water works just seemed to keep coming. She finally worked up the courage to ask, "Are you dying?"

Granny inhaled sharply. "Beck let that one slip, eh?"

"Oh, Granny." Alyssa crumpled into her arms and sobbed. She mopped at her face with a cloth napkin Granny handed her. "The cancer again?"

"Yes, love." Granny squeezed her. "It's all through me this time."

"Can't you do radiation and chemo? Please?" Her voice squeaked but she didn't care.

"No. I'm done. It's my time to go. I'm just worried about you."

Alyssa hung her head and studied the pattern in the bedspread. She wanted to reassure Granny she'd be fine, but she was going to be so alone. Maryn had betrayed her. Beck thought she'd betrayed him. Her dad had obviously had some part in this mess and she'd never have a relationship with him or her mom. All she had were her friends from girls' camp years ago, but most of them lived across the country and she wasn't as close to them emotionally as she wished she could be. Granny couldn't leave her. She couldn't.

"That's it! I'm done with this bull schmack." Granny slammed her palm on the side table. "We are going after him and he is going to believe you didn't do this. You need Beck. He promised me he'd take care of you."

135

"Oh, Granny." Alyssa shook her head. "He'll never forgive me. I told you I took pictures of him years ago. He's going to think that article is right and I have been stalking him for years and just waiting for this opportunity to snare him. I still don't understand why he mentioned my dad. Is he somehow involved?" She had the magazine open on her bed. If nothing else, she had these pictures of the two of them. She traced a finger across Beck's face.

Granny grabbed her hand and tilted Alyssa's chin up. "Beck is too good of a man to not give you a chance to explain. If your dad's involved, I'll kick his butt myself."

"I've tried to explain to Beck. I've sent texts, left voice messages. He's," she gulped, wiped at her face, and continued, "he's not responding."

"You have to do it face to face." She stood. "Pack your crap. We're flying out of here tonight." Granny hurried from the room, slamming the door behind her.

Alyssa stood and retrieved her suitcases from the closet, sighing. There was no use fighting Granny, but she didn't see how Beck would ever forgive her. Him being angry at her was awful enough, but the ache his absence created threatened to ruin her.

Chapter Twenty-two

Beck's oldest sister, Anna, stormed into his office and slapped several photographs onto his desk. Beck stared at the pictures of him and his sister leaving his parents' funeral. He knew the paparazzi had exploited his situation after their deaths, but he'd tried to ignore the pictures. Especially this series that All About Truth magazine had used to claim the family was being ripped apart because the will named him as the executor of the estate. He studied the first one for a minute and knew by the way the grief had been captured on both of their faces, this was an expert photographer. He didn't even have to ask who. It all tied in perfectly with what the recent magazine article about he and Alyssa had claimed.

"Looks like Miss Armsworth *has* been stalking you for some time."

Beck shook his head. "Are you serious?" His voice cracked and he hated himself for it. Alyssa wasn't the person he'd fallen in love with. It was almost like burying a loved one. His stomach had hurt less when he'd taken a jab on the ice. He glanced out the wall of windows at the view of Grand Park. Usually the glimpse of green and the wading pool was soothing, but not today.

These pictures were just more proof that Alyssa and her dad were as shady and corrupt as his family believed. He'd reported the threats by Alyssa's father to the FBI and they had Beck's phone tapped, hoping Gary would try to collect the money he'd demanded and they could catch him in blackmail. The FBI admitted the guy had never been caught, but he'd been on their radar for a while. Peter had already succeeded in forcing him out of the magazine ownership, so there was that small victory.

Beck kept trying to push away the memories of Alyssa's sweetness, her laughter, her kiss, but at night he struggled. She visited his dreams and haunted him. He still couldn't believe that the Alyssa and Ellie he thought he knew could do this to him.

Anna came around the desk and rested her hand on his shoulder. "I'm sorry."

Beck stood and hugged her. He cleared his throat and muttered, "Thanks for always being here for me."

She nodded. "You're taking this really hard."

"I know." He pulled away and sat back down, stacking the magnets in some desk toy Shelby had given him for Christmas. "I thought she was different."

"Oh, little bro." Anna stroked his hair like his mom used to do.

Beck was afraid he was going to cry. He missed his mom. He missed Alyssa. Thank heavens for his sisters. For a moment, he wondered if Ellie was still with Alyssa. She'd played him, but he didn't like the thought of her being alone and hurting.

"We're barbecuing tonight at my house," Anna said brightly. "You in?"

"Sure." What else was he going to do after work? He'd already lifted so many weights this morning he was going to be sore for days.

"Bring potato salad."

"From the deli?"

"Don't tease me. Your homemade. With extra pickles."

"Are you expecting again?" She always craved his potato salad when she was pregnant.

Anna reddened and walked away. "Just bring it."

The door slammed and Beck found a genuine smile on his face.

She obviously wanted to wait for the barbecue to announce. He was thrilled at the idea of another niece or nephew. The smile left his face as he thought of Alyssa and her desire for a houseful of boys. He wondered what she was doing right now. He glanced down at the picture of him and Anna and his stomach tightened. Everything had been an act. Alyssa had known who he was from day one, and she'd probably connived a way to stay at the same bed and breakfast as him. Someone had stolen his itinerary, after all. The bed and breakfast wasn't on it, but if hackers could steal that, they could get the real plans somehow.

Could Ellie really have been in on it? The thought sickened him, but she had to have been. She could tell if a man was worth his weight in gold? She wanted him to take care of her granddaughter because she was dying of cancer? Ha. Everything they'd said had been a lie.

He stood and stalked to his office door, slamming his way out. "Linli, I'm leaving for the day."

Her dark brows arched. "At two o'clock?"

He nodded, but couldn't explain. The drive home passed in a blur of pain. Alyssa and Ellie's betrayal. How much he missed his parents and his little brother and wished they could be here for tonight's barbecue. Why couldn't they be here, be a part of Anna and Shelby's children's lives? Sadly, he'd never have children of his own. Darkness washed over him and he found himself in the enormous shop his dad had built under the suspended five-car garage. The motorcycles gleamed. The cleaning service did a nice job. He ran his hand over several handlebars. He hadn't ridden since the day of the accident with his brother. He'd told his dad to get rid of the motorcycles, but they seemed to soothe his father, not bring the awful memories they did to Beck.

He climbed on a Lauge Jensen and shook his head. He should sell all of them. This bike alone was worth half a million dollars.

Ridiculous when that money could be used to help so many. He'd held onto these in memory of his dad, but maybe it was time to let them go. Let go of the pain and the memories of the crashes.

For some reason, he couldn't resist starting the motorcycle. It purred underneath him and he eased it toward one of the garage doors. The door slid open automatically. Beck slowly rode through his Laguna Beach neighborhood, the coastline at his side. He reached the highway and reveled in the potency beneath him. It seemed to make all the pain go away. As always, he understood his dad more than he wanted to admit. He revved the engine, just to feel the power, the lure of nothing being able to stop him while on this bike.

He was on Laguna Canyon Road almost before he realized it, taking the turns, remembering the awfulness of that night, but also realizing how freeing it was to ride. The wind rushing through his hair. The sheer power of the bike making him feel like he could conquer anything.

Flying over a hill, he noticed a few seconds too late the two cars racing toward him. The MDX was in his lane and there was nowhere for Beck to go. He swerved to the side, his tires caught the gravel and spun out. The motorcycle screamed toward the edge of the road. He gripped the handlebars between his slick palms before deciding, his only chance was to jump. He pushed off with his feet and hands, airborne and not sure if he was going to fly over the cliff with his motorcycle or eat gravel. At that moment he realized, he'd never put a helmet on.

Chapter Twenty-three

It took them a day and a half to get a flight to Los Angeles and then it was a miserable all through the night traveling experience. After Alyssa forced Granny to admit she needed to rest from their redeye flight, they slept until late afternoon at a Four Seasons Hotel on the south end of Orange County. Granny woke starving and ready to go to battle for Alyssa.

"First of all we're getting some food, then we're going to rip Maryn's head off and she's going to tell us where to find Beck, then we're going to get your man."

Alyssa called the concierge and asked for sandwiches and fruit to be sent up and a taxi to be ready in half an hour. She knew how Granny liked things done and she still got nauseous thinking of Granny losing her battle with cancer. Alyssa would do anything for her.

Maryn had sent numerous apologetic texts, claiming it wasn't her fault. Alyssa hoped it wasn't. She had too few close friends to lose the one she'd been through so much with, but at the same time she knew what Maryn was willing to do to succeed.

They arrived at Maryn's apartment in Echo Park. Alyssa had liked living in this area. Maryn hadn't found a new roommate since Alyssa left for Hawaii. They'd talked about living together again, but now who knew what would happen.

Granny tottered up to the door and pounded on it.

Maryn swung the door open wide and held her arms wider. Her

blonde hair was in a messy bun but she would look gorgeous with no hair. She was closer to Granny's size than Alyssa's. "Friend! I'm so happy you're here. I'm so sorry about this nightmare."

Alyssa shook her head and took a step back. The betrayal was still too strong to just forgive, forget, and air kiss.

"You're not sorry yet," Granny said, sticking her face in front of Maryn.

"Granny!" Maryn squealed. "I haven't seen you in forever."

"Well, you're not going to be happy to see me now," Granny declared.

Maryn frowned. "Come on, we can all think positive thoughts and be happy to see each other. Crap happens, but we can get past it."

"No happy thoughts and no getting past the crap. You're going to tell us where Beck lives and then get the heck out of our lives." Granny tucked her arms under her surgically-assisted bosom and thrust her small chin out.

"Granny, Alyssa." Maryn hung her head. "Don't be cruel to your girl. They tricked me too."

"Like we're going to believe *that*," Granny said.

Alyssa was torn. Maryn had been her best friend for so many years. Deep inside, she didn't believe Maryn would do this to her, but the proof was right in the magazine that she had stuffed in her purse. She just never thought Maryn would offer her best friend up as a sacrifice to advance her career.

"You want Beck to believe you'd never spear him in the back like that, right?" Maryn stared straight at Alyssa with her wide jade-colored eyes. Alyssa cringed at the reference to Beck. He probably hated her.

"Well, then give me a chance to explain so you can explain it to him. And maybe you'll realize that *I'm* the victim here." Her mouth drooped.

"How much did you get paid to be the victim?" Alyssa spat out.

"I didn't take it and I quit working for that magazine."

Alyssa straightened. She studied her friend. Maryn's eyes were clear and full of compassion. She was telling the truth.

"Please." Maryn stepped back from the door. "Come in so we can talk."

Granny stalked past Maryn. "Fine, you've got five minutes. We've got to get to Beck and fix this mess. So make it snappy!"

Maryn nodded and looked at Alyssa. Alyssa slowly walked to the micro-suede couch and sat down next to Granny. Maryn perched on the edge of a recliner next to them and started talking fast, "I wrote my article without your names in it or any clues that would bus-roll you or Beckham, most of the article was quotes from Nikki and Holly about their richy relationships, but I guess the magazine had done some investigative work of their own. They knew about our friendship, they had the information on Beckham that I had, and they must've dug up our connection to those pictures of Beckham and his sister."

She sighed and continued. "They sent a photographer to Hawaii. He took a bunch of pictures and used a parabolic microphone to listen into a couple of conversations at night. They pieced it all together, made you into some stalker, and voila." She hung her head. "Apparently your dad is involved. From what I could find out, he's part-owner of the magazine now. Since I'd already quit I couldn't get the dirt I needed to see how involved he is. I'm so sorry. I would never scum-slam you like that."

Alyssa gave herself a few seconds to sort out what she felt. Granny went on a tirade about how she was going to kick Gary's butt all over California for a few minutes then fell miraculously silent. Alyssa reached over and covered Maryn's hand with hers. "I believe you."

Maryn looked up with tears cresting her tanned cheeks. She

stood, pulling Alyssa up, and hugging her tightly. "I needed to hear that so bad. You're my best girl and I am going to make this all up to you, I promise."

Granny gave them a few seconds then interrupted, "Okay, okay, enough of the blubbering. So how do we find Beck and how do we convince him that Alyssa's innocent?"

Maryn and Alyssa pulled apart. Maryn bit her lip. "I have all his dirt, work and home addresses. What if I come with you and show him the correspondence from the magazine?"

"Sounds good." Granny stood and pulled her phone out. "First I'm going to set Gary straight. Then we'll go to battle, girls."

Chapter Twenty-four

Beck remembered the pain. The every inch of your body aching kind of pain that he'd had after the accident with his brother all those years ago. This time there wasn't the guilt to go along with the cuts and bruises. He would've preferred this recovery, if he could stop thinking about Alyssa. He'd gone the rounds with his sisters. They were like a couple of overprotective hens, pecking away at everything Alyssa had done as if by ripping her apart they could protect their baby chick. Beck really didn't want to be their baby chick and he found himself sticking up for Alyssa. Even though he didn't have much hope that she was innocent, he missed her every minute of the much-too long hours of sitting in a hospital bed.

Anna swept into the room, looking perfectly put together as usual in a silky blouse and fitted skirt.

"How does a mom of wild boys dress nice?"

"I only doll up when I leave the house. At home it's sweats and T-shirts."

Beck laughed then held his chest to stop the movement he'd created. Luckily, he held in the ouch.

"Oh, bud." Anna came over and swept the hair from his forehead. "You're hurting bad."

"I'm fine. Doc says I can go home tomorrow."

"Really?" Anna glanced over his battered body. Luckily the concussion had been the worst of his injuries. Everything was bruised and scraped, but the only broken bone was his left arm. He could live without a left arm for a bit.

"He said the CAT scans are looking good, told me if I walked to the nurse's station and back he'd release me tomorrow." He grinned. "I walked it a few times to prove I was ready."

"Good boy. Peter will take great care of the boys and I'll come stay with you for a few days."

He shook his head. "No, you won't. I'm not a child."

Anna raised an eyebrow. "Prove that by wearing a helmet next time."

Beck groaned. "There won't be a next time. I'm selling the motorcycles."

"I'm surprised you held onto them this long." She nodded her approval.

"They reminded me of Dad." Beck's lips twisted and he focused on the monitors next to his bed.

"I know. It's hard to let go of anything that keeps them alive." She sat carefully on the edge of his bed. "Any other drastic plans you have?"

Beck studied her for a minute. "I'd like to talk to Alyssa." He wasn't sure what he'd say to her, but he couldn't keep living like this with the doubts and the questions and the hope that maybe, just maybe she was innocent and maybe, just maybe she missed him as much as he missed her.

Anna exhaled slowly but nodded. "I don't want her to have the chance to hurt you again."

"I'm a big boy."

"Yeah, unfortunately you grew up and don't want to listen to your sister anymore."

"Did I ever listen?"

"Touchè."

146

Chapter Twenty-five

Alyssa's heart thumped so loud she was sure everybody could hear it as she, Granny, and Maryn walked out the elevator and through the swinging glass doors with a beautiful emblem of Jordan's Buds stenciled on one door and Taylor Enterprises on the other. No one had answered at Beck's house. She'd almost stopped her search when she saw how ostentatious his home was. Had he been playing a role in Maui? Was he really the man she thought he was? Luckily, Granny and Maryn were there to remind her Beck was nothing like her father and he'd inherited the house from his parents. It wasn't like he'd designed a mansion just for himself, he probably had a lot of memories tied up in all that square footage.

In the lobby of Beck's offices, a beautiful woman smiled a welcome from a huge mahogany wood desk. Her black hair was short and spiky and her slanted eyes gave her an exotic look. "May I help you?"

Alyssa stepped forward, but Granny pre-empted her. "We need to talk to Beck and we're not taking no for an answer."

The woman's eyes narrowed, she glanced from Alyssa to Granny. "Mr. Taylor is not in the office today. Can I take a message for you?"

Alyssa's rapidly beating heart sank. She'd been thinking through all the things she would say to Beck and how he would react, but he wasn't at his house and he wasn't here. Had he already left the country on a humanitarian trip? How was she going to find him? Would he call her back if she left a message? Doubtful. The first dozen messages hadn't gotten any response after all.

"I don't think you understand," Granny said. "We're *very* good friends of Beck's. He'll be unhappy if we don't get to see him."

The woman's smile thinned. "If you are *very* good friends of Beck's, you should be able to call him on his cell phone."

"I've tried," Alyssa burst out. "He hasn't returned my calls. I'm worried something's wrong." The something that was wrong was Beck didn't want to talk to her.

The woman studied Alyssa and she held her gaze. "You didn't hear about the accident?"

Alyssa wobbled and would've fallen, but Maryn wrapped an arm around her waist.

"No," she whispered.

A man walked out of a back office and nodded politely to them before focusing on the secretary. "Is everything okay, Linli?"

She gestured to them. "These ladies claim to be Beck's friends. They haven't been able to get a hold of him since the accident."

He turned to them, compassion radiating from his dark eyes as he focused in on Alyssa. "I'm sorry." Then his eyes widened and he said, "Oh, you're..."

"Is Beck okay?" Alyssa asked, preempting him turning them away.

The man swallowed and nodded. "He's improving. I really think you should go now." He gestured toward the door.

"Please," Alyssa took a step forward. "I just need to know if he's all right."

The man's eyes softened a bit. "He'll recover."

"W-what happened?" The words squeaked past her dry throat.

"Motorcycle accident."

A wave of darkness swept over Alyssa. She heard Maryn and Granny screaming but couldn't respond as the floor came rushing up to meet her.

Alyssa came around quickly. The man escorted her to a leather couch and then he and Linli listened as Granny and Maryn explained the entire story. Silence descended on the group for a few seconds after Maryn ran out of arguments for Alyssa's innocence. Finally, the man cleared his throat and said, "I'm Peter, Beck's brother-in-law."

Alyssa sat up. "Anna's husband?"

He nodded, focusing on her for several uncomfortable seconds. "Beck fell hard for you."

Her entire world lit up. "He did?"

Peter sighed. "From the look on your face and the way you responded to his accident, either you're the most fabulous actress I've ever met, or you fell for him too."

"I love him, Peter." She held his gaze, begging him to believe her.

He pursed his lips and studied her as the seconds ticked by, finally he shook his head. Alyssa about cried out. He wasn't going to help them. How was she ever going to find Beck? She'd have to start by canvassing the hospitals in the area.

"My wife is going to skin me for this," Peter interrupted her thoughts, "but I'm going to take you to Beck."

Alyssa released all her breath. Too weak to cheer, she blinked at the moisture building behind her eyes. Her throat was tight, but she managed to whisper, "Thank you."

He shrugged. "I hope it all works out for you, Alyssa, but you should know that Beck and his sisters are going to be much harder to convince than me."

Granny grinned at him. "You're just a sappy sucker, aren't you?"

Peter laughed. "I think we'll sic you on Anna and let Alyssa convince Beck."

Granny rubbed her hands together and licked her lips. "I just love being part of a good cat fight."

Maryn cackled. "This is why I miss you so much, Granny."

The tears Alyssa had been fighting streamed out. Maryn didn't know about Granny's impending death.

"Be nice to my wife," Peter admonished.

"Okay, take all my fun away." Granny winked at Peter.

The drive to the hospital was less than twenty minutes but it felt like two hours. Alyssa rode with Peter while Maryn and Granny followed in Maryn's car. Peter explained Beck had a concussion, broken arm, and numerous scrapes and abrasions. It made her sick to think of Beck being in pain. She wondered how he was dealing with the accident emotionally. Was he mourning his brother and parents all over again? She wanted to comfort him, but didn't know if he would even want to see her. Would he forgive her? She could only picture the anger in his blue eyes when she last saw him.

They parked at the UC Irvine Medical Center and walked for what felt like another two hours through the nicely-landscaped walkways, past security, and then down hallway after hallway. Even Granny was silent as if she understood the seriousness of the upcoming interchange.

Peter talked to the nurse and then she buzzed them through the double doors. "This is his room," he said a few seconds later.

Alyssa took a deep breath and faced everyone. "I'd like to talk to him alone."

"But what if he doesn't believe you?" Maryn asked. "I have all the proof."

Alyssa gnawed at her cheek. "If he doesn't believe me, the proof doesn't matter."

Peter nodded. "It's between you two." He gave her arm a squeeze. "Good luck."

Alyssa smiled up at him, wishing that things were different and she could enjoy getting to know Beck's family with Beck by her side, instead of him being on the other side of that door and probably hating her.

The door creaked open and a beautiful dark-haired woman exited, closing it behind her. "Peter!" She went straight into his arms and gave him a quick kiss. "I didn't know you were going to come visit. Who has the boys?"

"My mom took them to a movie, so I went in to work for a bit."

"Oh, that woman's a saint."

Peter laughed and then turned her to face all of them. "Sweetheart, this is Alyssa, Maryn, and Granny Ellie."

As soon as her gaze connected with Alyssa's, her smile turned to a scowl. "You? How dare you come here?"

Peter tightened his grip on Anna's arms and pulled her close. "Alyssa had no part in that article. You need to listen to Maryn's side of the story while Alyssa talks to Beck."

"You think I'm going to let that paparazzi be alone with my brother!"

"Don't you dare call my grandbaby paparazzi." Granny thrust her face in front of Anna's. "She is an angel who has done nothing wrong and furthermore, she's in love with your brother and you're just going to have to deal with that!"

Anna's eyes spit fire. She edged toward the doorway, blocking Alyssa from entering. "This woman has hurt my brother more than anything besides the deaths of our parents and brother. You have no right to ask any of us to deal with that."

Pain rushed through Alyssa. Her chest tightened. She'd hurt Beck that horribly?

"Oh, love." Peter hugged his wife close. "The reason it hurt Beck so badly is because he loves her, but he's going to forgive her for the same reason."

A powerfully-built woman with spiky gray hair rushed toward the group. "You all need to keep it down or take it outside."

"We'll go outside," Peter said. He kept Anna in his embrace and started moving toward the elevator.

Maryn and Granny followed.

Peter looked back at Alyssa and gestured with his chin toward Beck's hospital door. "Go," he mouthed.

Alyssa didn't need to be told twice. While the nurses shepherded the group away, she slipped into Beck's hospital room, but someone was already there. Belle leaned over Beck's bed. Alyssa couldn't see much other than Belle's backside in her usual tight attire, this time a business suit of some sort, but she could hear—Belle moaning softly and the unmistakable sound of kissing.

She pivoted and raced from the room. Tears streamed down her face as she waited for the elevator and ran down the hallways and then into the parking lot. Granny and Maryn were up ahead. Alyssa didn't know how to face Beck's family. His brother-in-law had been so kind. Alyssa still wanted a chance to talk to Beck, but not with that woman there. The hope drained from her as she thought of Belle kissing him so... loudly. It made her want to gag.

She hurried away from the group toward a water feature, wanting nothing more than to hide and cry her eyes out. Maybe Beck had always planned on getting back together with Belle and Hawaii was just a fling for him, or maybe Belle had swooped back in when Alyssa had broken Beck's heart with her betrayal. Some part of her knew she deserved this, but she didn't know how she'd survive it.

"Alyssa."

Crap, Maryn had seen her. She turned and forced herself to wait as the group caught up to her.

"Is everything okay?" It was Beck's sister, Anna.

The softly-spoken question was Alyssa's undoing. Tears poured now and she couldn't keep up with the flow as she dashed them off her cheeks. "No. Yes. It's fine. Please tell Beck I'm sorry and I wish him and Belle the best."

Anna's eyes narrowed and she opened her mouth to speak but Alyssa couldn't take any more. She whirled on her heel and sprinted toward Maryn's car.

Chapter Twenty-six

Beck felt the pressure of lips on his. "Alyssa," he murmured, but then he realized the smell and feel was all wrong. The perfume was too strong and the lips were hard and demanding. He pushed the woman away with his right arm and forced his gritty lids to open. "Belle! What are you doing with your tongue in my mouth?" Gross. He needed mouthwash.

"Oh, poor baby." She leaned down and he had to look at the monitors to avoid seeing everything that expensive surgery had blessed her with. "I came as soon as I heard. Can I get you anything?"

"No." Beck shook his head and closed his eyes. "I'm just really tired."

"Go ahead and rest. I told Anna I'd watch over you while she grabbed some food."

Aw, crap. How was he going to get rid of her? He heard her settle into the chair by his bed and finally opened his eyes, focusing on her face as he already knew too well what her body looked like in the form-fitting outfits she always wore. "I really appreciate you coming, but I'm not very good company right now."

"You're always good company for me," she said. Her eyes got that wicked gleam they used to get when she'd talk him into doing something neither of their parents wanted them to. Before she turned into such a brat, they used to be friends. "I'm sorry about that gold digger. Alyssa, was it?"

Beck swallowed. "She's not a gold digger."

154

Belle stroked his arm. "Beck. You're too good. Always being so kind about everyone." She pressed her firm chest against his arm. "I'm here for you, baby. We can be together again. You know I don't have any agenda but wanting to be with you."

Beck pulled his arm away. "It didn't work for us five years ago and it's not going to work now." He'd always tried to keep a good relationship with Belle and her family, but he really wasn't up for her games today. He wanted a real woman who cared about his causes and cared about people. He'd seen the way Belle treated anyone she thought was beneath her. The thought of taking her on a humanitarian trip almost made him laugh out loud. Taking Alyssa anywhere was like a dream come true. Belle didn't hold a candle to Alyssa's beauty, compassion, talent, or the desire Beck had for her. As soon as he got out of this hospital bed, he needed to find Alyssa. He knew those stories sensationalized the truth. It was time to get over his hurt feelings and find out what Alyssa was really about.

"Give us a chance again?" Belle begged, her bottom lip jutting out. The look was cute on his three-year old niece.

"No." Beck said. He sat up, feeling stronger than he had since the accident. "You and I are not a couple and we never will be, but thanks for coming by."

Belle's mouth dropped open. She closed it, narrowed her eyes, and stood. "Don't expect any more contributions from Daddy."

"I hope your father doesn't base his charity on what his spoiled daughter wants, but if that's the way it's going to be, I can live with that."

Belle whirled and stomped from the room. Beck closed his eyes, relief pouring through him. He didn't have to tread lightly around her anymore. He hoped he hadn't just lost a major contributor as that wasn't fair to the children, but the money he received from selling all of his motorcycles would fund most of those programs for a few years.

If he had to, he'd sell some of his investment rentals, not build some of the commercial buildings they had scheduled, or pull some money out of stocks.

He took a sip of water and paged the nurse. "Do you have any gum?"

"Gum?" she asked.

"Breath mints? Mouth wash? I've got a nasty taste in my mouth I want to get rid of." He wanted to be done with anything that reminded him of Belle and the fake relationship they used to have. Then maybe he could fall asleep and dream of Alyssa again.

"I'll see what I can find."

Beck relaxed against the stiff pillows and smiled. The sooner he got the taste of Belle off of him the better. Now if only he could have a taste of Alyssa. That would cure every ache and pain.

Chapter Twenty-seven

Alyssa only made it halfway across the parking lot. Her stupid foot wasn't supporting her very well today. Anna caught her and latched onto her arm. Her blue eyes were filled with fire. "If you care about my brother, why are you running away?"

"Belle," she managed to get out before sniffling like an idiot. She pressed the back of her hand to her nose and blinked quickly.

"In all the commotion I forgot about her. What was she doing?" Anna asked.

"In the hospital room kissing Beck."

Anna shook her head and nodded to her husband as the group caught up with them. "Belle's taking advantage of the situation as usual. She acted all nice, said she'd sit with Beck while I ran to get something to eat. That woman makes my skin crawl."

"I know what I saw," Alyssa insisted.

"A comatose man being kissed by a predator?" Anna asked. Her lip curled in derision. Alyssa hoped it was for Belle and not her.

"Beck was asleep when I left him," Anna continued. "And I can promise you he has no interest in Belle. Our dads always tried to push them together, and Belle tried every trick she had, but Beck was never interested in Miss Fake and Tight."

"Never?"

Anna shook her head, her eyes filling with compassion. "He tried to date her for Dad's sake, but he knew she wasn't the one for him, knew it years before he met you."

"Do you think I am the..." Alyssa couldn't finish the question.

"Even when I tried to talk poorly about you, Beck didn't listen. You should see the look in his eyes when he talks about you."

Alyssa couldn't hide a smile.

"You should see how sappy they are together," Granny inserted.

Alyssa was amazed Granny had stayed quiet this long. Oh, she loved her Granny Ellie.

Anna tugged on Alyssa's arm. "How about you go see Beck and you two talk this out?"

"Okay," she whispered. She didn't know if she was brave enough to go back into that hospital room, but she and Beck at least deserved a chance to work through it. The walk back to the hospital and wait for the elevator were the longest she could remember. The entire group kept nudging and smiling. She would've faltered without the support. Finally, she was standing outside his door then a push from behind propelled her through it. Granny or Anna, she wasn't sure.

Beck sat up on the bed. His eyes widened. "Alyssa." He swallowed and then whispered, "You came."

Alyssa wanted to rush to his side and put a kiss on each of his bruises, but the somber look on his face held her in place. "Oh, Beck. I'm so sorry you got hurt."

He gave her a ghost of a smile. "I'll be fine."

"Will you?"

He inhaled and then released the breath slowly. "Someday."

The slight catch in his voice prompted her to take a tentative step forward. "What if... what if I won't be fine?"

He studied her face. "Did you get hurt?"

"Yes," she whispered.

"How?" His brow furrowed and for just an instant he was that guy again, the guy who protected her from the druggie, kissed her until she forgot the world, and would right her every wrong.

"When you wouldn't believe me that I would never have betrayed you with those pictures and that article. It hurt me, right here." She placed a hand on her heart.

Beck closed his eyes for half a second. When he opened them she thought she saw a glimmer of hope. "Are you telling me I can trust you?"

"Just like I can trust that you weren't kissing Belle willingly."

Beck's eyes filled with disgust. "You can. I got rid of her."

"I had nothing to do with that article, Beck." She paused and amended, "Well, I did take those pictures years ago when I was in an awful spot and really needed some money. I didn't know how they were going to twist them to hurt you. And Maryn did ask me to secure one date with you when you came to Hawaii, but she promised our names and pictures wouldn't be in it. I didn't want to do it, but I figured I'd get the date to help Maryn and that would be that, but then I fell for you." She squeezed her hands together, unable to meet his gaze. "And the Billionaire Bride Pact is true, but I never wanted to fulfill it. They called me the dark side of the pact."

Beck chuckled and she finally allowed herself to look at him. "The dark side of the pact?"

"Wait until you meet my friends."

He smirked at her and then said, "It's okay about the article, Alyssa."

"I need you to know I would never hurt you on purpose."

"Why?"

"Because." She bit at her lip and found herself unable to hold his gaze. "I've fallen in love with you, Beck."

"Alyssa, please look at me."

She looked up and saw his blue eyes were brighter than normal. "Even if you had stalked me for years and written that entire article, I would forgive you, because... I love you too."

A whimper escaped from her throat. He lifted his un-casted arm and she rushed to his side, sinking onto the hospital bed. Beck pulled her against his chest. "Oh, Alyssa, I missed you."

She glanced up at him. "There's so much I need to tell you, to explain."

"Later," his voice had gone low and husky. His head lowered toward hers and Alyssa didn't mind waiting to explain.

Chapter Twenty-eight

Beck squatted behind a potted plant at the exclusive Newport Beach restaurant, 21 Oceanfront. "My thighs are killing me," he muttered.

"Hush," Granny said, not appearing to be struggling at all, maybe because she was so small to begin with and didn't have as far to squat. It was hard to imagine that she was really sick and dying. "He can't see us until the perfect moment."

"We could find an easier spot to hide."

"Are you trying to take all the fun out of an old lady's final few days?"

Beck wasn't sure what was fun about squatting for over ten minutes, but he didn't want to upset Granny right now. That she was willing to go along with his plan to teach her "punk son" a lesson was crazy to him. Beck's parents would never have sided with someone against him, but he also wasn't a crook who would prostitute his own daughter.

A smile lit his lips as he thought of Alyssa. After this was over, he was going to take her to dinner and enjoy every kiss she let him steal. After his arm was fully healed and he had clearance from his doctor to leave the country, he and Alyssa could start planning trips to help Jordan's Buds.

"There he is." Granny clamped onto his right arm, her nails digging into his skin. "You ready?"

"Yep." Beck started to rise, but Granny pulled him back down.

"Wait until he's seated and staring at his menu."

Gary sat at a corner table with a twenty-something blonde. He trailed his fingers up her side then copped a discreet squeeze of her breast before lifting his menu. Beck took that as his cue and stood. Granny shakily rose and Beck knew she'd been lying that the squat hadn't affected her. He held onto her elbow and escorted her around the pot and toward Alyssa's dad.

The blonde spotted them first. She winked at Beck. Her eyes traveled up and down his frame. "Hello," she said breathlessly

"We aren't here to be seduced by a floozy," Granny shot out.

Gary's head jerked up. "Mother." He stood and reached out a hand to her.

Ellie gave him an imperious glare. "We aren't here to reconnect either. Beck, do it."

Gary lowered his hand and looked warily at Beck. "Beckham, good to see you again."

"Wish I could say the same," Beck countered.

Gary's eyebrows drew together but he didn't comment. He did remain standing. His eyes wavering between Granny and Beck.

"I could have you arrested for blackmail," Beck said, "but your mother cares enough about you to keep you out of jail."

"You have no proof."

"Oh, but I do. Several men, in fact, have come forward to admit to your blackmail and shady business dealings. Maryn is pretty unreal at research and she's got a fabulous new job with The Rising Star."

Gary's eyebrows shot up at the mention of Maryn and the top magazine in the nation.

"An article will be running tomorrow about the different blackmail techniques you've employed. You won't be getting much business after tomorrow and there's another thing that will be printed in that article."

"What's that?" Gary snarled. His face red and his fists clenched.

"This." Beck stepped aside and Granny slapped Gary soundly across the cheek. He whirled back and grabbed at his cheek. Lights flashed as a photographer from The Rising Star clicked several shots.

"Don't you ever come near my granddaughter or her future husband again," Granny commanded. "Beck wanted to knock your lights out and I still might let him, but I didn't want you to have any chance of looking like a defenseless old man. When the granny knocks you out, it just shows what a wimp you are."

Beck wrapped his arm securely around Granny's shoulder. "And I have no problem with my name being splashed all over the article tomorrow and neither do the other men you tried to blackmail after you tried to prostitute your own daughter to them."

They turned and walked away. Beck felt a huge amount of satisfaction until he realized Granny's thin shoulders were trembling under his arm. He stopped outside the restaurant. "Granny? You okay?"

She wiped at her eyes and shook her head. "It's a tough thing to realize that your only child is a complete piece of crap."

Beck nodded. He couldn't even imagine. "But look how amazing your granddaughter is and she tells me all the time that's thanks to you."

Granny's smile wobbled but it was there. "*She* is amazing."

"I've heard that you can't judge your parenting by your children. It's your grandchildren that show if you've really done a good job."

"Oh, Beck." She hugged him. "I knew I liked you. What do you say we go find my beautiful granddaughter and I let you buy us both dinner?"

"That's the second best plan you've had tonight."

Chapter Twenty-nine

Granny took a turn for the worse not long after they confronted Gary. Alyssa knew it was coming, but still wasn't sure how she was going to survive without Granny.

Beck moved Granny Ellie into his guest house, but she made them both promise that they would, "Bury me in Idaho so all my friends can come blubber over me and there won't be so many darn people and traffic around. My rotting corpse needs fresh air." Beck laughed at her, but Alyssa could hardly crack a smile.

Hospice had been coming for a week when Beck insisted Alyssa move in to the guest house also so she wouldn't miss a minute with Granny.

"Today's the day," Granny declared or rather whispered. It was a beautiful, sunny Thursday.

"The day for what?" Alyssa asked.

"For me to go home. Call Beck for me, will you my sweet?"

"Sure." Alyssa dialed Beck's number with shaking fingers.

"Good morning, love," Beck greeted her.

"Can you please come over? She's... asking for you."

"Sure."

Several minutes later Beck appeared, dressed in a button down shirt and slacks like he'd been ready to head into work. He and Alyssa had decided to wait on their humanitarian trip until things were settled with Granny.

"Beck," Granny's voice was soft as a warm breeze, like it was almost too much effort to even use it.

He leaned down and kissed her cheek then sat next to Alyssa at the side of her bed. "How are you feeling, Ellie?"

"Not worth the bullet to shoot me with." She cracked a small smile.

Beck smiled with her. Alyssa wiped away another round of tears.

"You know I held on until we found you," Ellie said to Beck.

Beck nodded. "I know."

"You promised me."

Beck focused on Alyssa and smiled. He wrapped an arm around her shoulders. She leaned into him, needing his strength.

"Thank you. This old nag can die in peace now." She turned to Alyssa. "I love you, sweetheart. You're the best of me."

Tears ran unchecked down Alyssa's face as she kissed Granny's soft cheek. "I love you," she choked out. "Thank you for always being there for me."

"I'm so proud of you," Granny whispered. She looked over Alyssa's shoulder and grinned. "Hubba Bubba. Guess the Lord knew who my favorite was." Her eyes closed with a satisfied smile on her lips and her chest stopped moving.

Alyssa's tears kept coming, but the devastation she felt didn't completely rip her apart. Beck pulled her against his chest and simply held her close while she cried and savored the warmth and peace in the room. Granny was gone and Alyssa knew she'd miss her every day, but she wasn't alone. She glanced up at Beck. She wouldn't ever be alone again.

He gently kissed her forehead. "Who was Hubba Bubba?"

Alyssa laughed in spite of herself and swiped a few tears away. "Her favorite husband. Big Polynesian. Awesome guy. My grandpa died when she was only twenty-eight. He was an Air Force pilot and was killed in Vietnam. Granny was married to Hubba Bubba for almost thirty years. Sadly, he loved to eat and died of a heart attack at sixty-five."

"That is sad. She's been through a lot, but she was an amazing lady."

"Yes, she was." Alyssa studied her grandmother's tiny body. The smile was still there. It was a beautiful thing to know she'd died so peaceful and was ready to be in heaven with those she loved.

Beck tenderly dried a tear from her face.

"Thank you," Alyssa whispered. "For taking care of her. For taking care of me."

"I'll always take care of you." Beck stroked her back, cradling her in his arms. Alyssa knew he was telling the truth.

Chapter Thirty

"Wow," Beck's husky voice came from the side.

Alyssa whirled to face him and flung herself into his arms. His cast had been removed several weeks ago and though his left arm was a bit thinner than his right, he seemed as strong and perfect as ever to her.

He kissed her thoroughly then held her back to gaze over the form-fitting blue dress. "Anna took you shopping?"

"She has a talent for it." She appreciated the way he looked in a dark gray suit that fit him extremely well.

"Yes, she does." He pulled her close again and trailed kisses up her neck to her cheek.

Alyssa couldn't contain the soft moan that escaped.

"I could kiss you all night," he whispered against the side of her lips, "but Anna would beat me if I missed her party."

"I'm a little awkward about all of this." She leaned into him, grateful for his solid strength.

"Why? Everyone will love you."

"Just because you love me, doesn't mean everyone else will."

He chuckled. "They will, believe me. I'm a tough judge and I love every part of you." He rubbed his hands down her back and kissed her until she wasn't sure which way was up.

Alyssa melted. Beck released her from the hug, but took her hand and gave her a smile that said he knew exactly how he affected her. She still wasn't sure why Anna had to throw a huge fancy party so she could meet all of Beck's friends and family before they left on their first humanitarian trip, but she'd go anywhere if Beck was there with her. He led her out the French doors at the rear of his house and down the patio steps. People were gathering around the beautiful yard, mostly next to the pool where there were appetizers before the dinner that Anna had organized. Maryn was flirting with a tall, good-looking man with skin like rich chocolate. Alyssa smiled, liking the contrast in coloring and size between the two and wishing she could snap a few pictures. She wished Granny could be here, but had a feeling she was here in spirit.

Beck tugged on her hand and Alyssa looked up at him. "What?"

"C'mere for a second." He drew her away from the people and around the edge of the house where a hedge and flower garden provided some privacy. Beck directed her to a bench and she sat down, arching back to study his face. She hadn't seen him this serious since that awful day in Hawaii when he left her.

"Is everything okay?"

Beck brushed a hand through his hair, ruining the perfectly gelled effect. Alyssa smiled, she loved his hair mussed.

"Anna is going to kill me." He paced in front of the bench. "We planned this all out, but..."

Alyssa stood. "Beck. You can tell me. I can help you with anything."

Beck turned to her and studied her face for a few seconds. He broke into a soft smile. "I know you can, love."

He helped her sit on the bench again and then sank down onto one knee in front of her. Alyssa's breath caught at the beauty of this man and how much she loved him.

"Anna organized this party to help me out. We had this elaborate scheme, which you and I will probably still have to pretend to go through or she'll skin me."

Alyssa laughed and touched his arm. "Beck. Whatever you and Anna had planned we can do. I don't want to upset her."

"No." He shook his head. "I love you Alyssa, and I want this to be our private moment, no matter how much Anna wants to be part of it." He withdrew a ring box from the jacket of his suit coat. His hands shook a little bit as he popped it open to reveal a gorgeous round diamond set in a simple gold band. The diamond was larger than Alyssa would've picked out, probably over two carats, but the simplicity of the setting was exactly what she would've wanted. It was stunning and screamed to her of Beck's love and devotion.

"Will you marry me?"

Alyssa stood and pulled him to his feet. She kissed him quickly on the mouth then encircled her arms around his neck. "Yes!"

He kissed her for several wonderful seconds until she forgot about the party and everything else in the world. He drew back and said, "Do you care if I wait to give you the ring until we do the big thing for Anna?"

"Beck, as long as I'm with you, I don't care what else happens."

He grinned. "Good, because I'm not letting you out of my sight."

They kissed until Anna found them and demanded they come join the party. Alyssa couldn't wipe the smile off her face as Beck's hand found hers and they followed Anna to the party. Whatever surprise Anna had planned for Beck to propose would be fun, but all that really mattered was being with him.

Additional Works By Cami Checketts

Sweet Romance

Tenderness and Terror Series
(Clean Romantic Thriller)

Clean Romantic Suspense

About the Author

Cami is a part-time author, part-time exercise consultant, part-time housekeeper, full-time wife, and overtime mother of four adorable boys. Sleep and relaxation are fond memories. She's never been happier.

Sign up for Cami's newsletter to receive a free ebook and information about new releases, discounts, and promotions here.

If you enjoyed *The Resilient One*, please consider posting a review on Amazon, Goodreads, or your personal blog. Thank you for helping to spread the word.

www.camichecketts.com

Excerpt from - The Passionate One

(A Billionaire Bride Pact Romance)

The Passionate One
by Jeanette Lewis

"I, Erin Marie Parker, do solemnly swear, that someday I'll marry a billionaire ...

OR I will have to sing the Camp Wallakee song (with the caws) at my wedding."

The Camp Wallakee girls all ended up on the same row at the wedding. Erin was the last to arrive and was greeted with a chorus of squeals and hugs. She took the seat on the end of the aisle and shifted to adjust the skirt of her silvery gray dress. After brushing her rose gold hair out of her eyes, she leaned forward and beamed down the row at her girls. It was as if no time at all had passed and they were kids at camp again - sharing care packages from home, riding the zip line into the lake, roasting marshmallows around the campfire, and telling creepy stories in the cabin with flashlights under their chins. Erin's stories were usually the best, probably because she had the best ear-splitting scream and she liked to spring it on them when they least expected it. She always had to tell her story last because the resulting chaos would usually bring in a counselor who would yell at them to go to sleep.

Erin looked again at the row of women sitting beside her. Okay, some things had changed. The scrawny, scabby knees were gone, as was most of the acne. And they'd all filled out - some more than others. Lindsey was beautiful with her enormous blue eyes and pouty lips; Taylor was still tall and skinny, but not all arms and legs anymore; and Holly looked polished and perfect in her designer dress and chestnut highlights.

To her right, MacKenzie sighed. "Isn't this beautiful?" she said to Erin.

Erin glanced around. "Yeah. But who gets married in a cemetery?" There was no denying that the West Laurel Hills Cemetery in Bala Cynwyd, Pennsylvania was a beautiful place. The grass was still green, but many of the trees were wearing their autumn colors and the splashes of red, yellow, orange, and brown created a nice contrast against the blue of the sky and the white and gray tones of the mausoleums and gravestones.

The aisle between the rows of transparent chairs was a carpet of autumn leaves, ending at the Louis Burk mausoleum It was pure Roman architecture with its ionic columns flanking a copper gate, weathered to a gray green patina and featuring a sorrowful maiden in a dramatic pose that brought a sweet ache to Erin's heart. The wide, low steps of the mausoleum were banked with flowers in shades of cranberry, pale pink, and ivory.

But still, a *cemetery?*

MacKenzie laughed. "That's Nikki. You didn't think she'd pick somewhere *normal*, did you?"

Erin couldn't say. Nikki had always been a little quirky, but Erin hadn't been privy to her wedding plans. In fact, she hadn't known Nikki was even engaged until she got the invitation in the mail. They'd all tried to keep in touch in the years following camp, but some were better at it than others, and their contact had become less and less frequent as they got older and busier. Erin could probably have remembered what each of her friends was doing now if pressed, but she'd have to think about it a little bit first.

Which was part of the reason she was so excited for the wedding. Taylor's wedding four years earlier didn't count because Taylor had eloped and hadn't invited anyone. This was the first time most of the girls had been together again and it was the perfect opportunity to catch up.

"Do you know the groom?" Erin asked MacKenzie.

"Not at all," MacKenzie shook her head. "But I hear he's loaded." She elbowed Holly, who sat on her other side. "Isn't that right?"

"What?" Holly looked up from her phone.

"Isn't Darrin super rich?" MacKenzie repeated.

Holly nodded. "I think he owns some kind of software company."

"Count it," Erin smiled in satisfaction. "We never said it had to be inherited money."

"What are you talking about?" Holly wrinkled her perfect brows.

"The Billionaire Bride Pact," Erin clarified. "Remember?"

"I do," MacKenzie put in.

Understanding dawned in Holly's eyes. "Oh, that's right. I forgot about that."

Erin glanced at Holly's left hand, where a diamond the size of a small Volkswagen glittered on her ring finger. "I guess it's lucky you found Josh then," she said, widening her eyes dramatically. "Or you'd get ... *the consequence.*" The Billionaire Bride Pact had been her idea – because *of course* it had – and the notion that anyone had simply forgotten about it rankled a bit.

Holly gave her a small, tight smile. "I guess."

"Do you know what these chairs are called?" MacKenzie said amid the sudden tension. She tapped the seat of her transparent chair with her long, pink fingernails. "Ghost chairs. Appropriate, no?"

Erin nodded, but her stomach was tight. Holly had always been hard to read and the two of them had clashed more than once at camp. Erin had had a talent for annoying her then and it looked like that hadn't changed.

She glanced down the aisle again, taking note of who was missing.

"Do you know if Kynley is coming?" Of all the Wallakee girls, Erin missed Kynley the most. Maybe it was because they had such similar personalities.

MacKenzie shook her head. "I'm sure she wanted to be here, but with her crazy touring schedule, she probably couldn't get away."

"What about Alyssa?"

"She's here, off taking pictures probably. Maryn's saving her a seat." MacKenzie nodded her head toward the empty seat at Maryn's side. Alyssa and Maryn had come to camp together; Erin wasn't surprised to see they were still close friends.

"What about Summer?"

MacKenzie rolled her eyes. "Who knows where Summer is? Probably sailing down The Vltava on a raft."

They laughed. If anyone could be found sailing down The Vltava on a raft, it would be Summer. "I'll bet she's wearing some funky bohemian outfit and has picked up at least one hunky Czech boyfriend, maybe more," Erin said, leaping into the fantasy.

"I'm guessing more," MacKenzie said.

There was a disturbance at the back and they all turned. The wedding party was getting into position.

"Don't you love weddings?" MacKenzie sighed, once it became obvious they weren't quite ready to start. "Holly, have you decided where yours will be yet?"

"Please have it outside," Erin urged. "Though maybe not in a cemetery."

"Ha! I'm getting married in the winter. Trust me, you do *not* want to be outside for very long in a Utah winter," Holly replied.

"But you could ride in on a sleigh, pulled by white horses," Erin said excitedly. She could almost see it. With her dark hair, Holly would make a beautiful winter bride. "The horses could have sleigh bells and you could wear a white fur cape and carry a bouquet of red roses, mistletoe, and *holly* berries. It's perfect!" She put her hand over her mouth and launched into her best Darth Vader wheeze, "it's your *destiny*."

Holly laughed. "Maybe I should hire you as my wedding consultant."

Erin shook her head, relaxing at the sound of Holly's laughter. "Not my gig. But I'll give you that idea for free."

They stopped talking as a pastor in a long black robe came down a side aisle, followed by a string quartet and a guitarist. The musicians took seats to the left of the mausoleum, while the pastor went to the steps. After a brief tuning, the guitarist began to play a series of chords and the quartet joined in soon after. Erin had expected *Canon in D* or some other wedding staple and was pleasantly surprised when they began to play *Can't Help Falling in Love*.

Everyone turned as the wedding party made its way down the carpet of autumn leaves, starting with Darrin and the best man. Darrin was not *quite* the kind of guy Erin would have imagined for Nikki, but he was cute in an understated way. His dark brown hair was newly trimmed, but still managed to look a bit shaggy, growing past his ears and long over his forehead. He had big, solemn brown eyes that made her think of a puppy poster, but when he smiled, they twinkled merrily at the guests. He was obviously having the time of his life.

Erin had missed yesterday's pre-wedding dinner. "Is he nice?" she whispered to MacKenzie as Darrin passed their row.

"He's great," MacKenzie replied. "They're so cute together."

Darrin and the best man reached the front and took their places at the pastor's side as the parents began their walk down the aisle. Next came Nikki's five bridesmaids in long gowns of varying shades of pink, wine, and cranberry. They were escorted by groomsmen in black suits with ties that matched the bridesmaid's dresses. Erin's eye fell on the second groomsman in line. He was tall, with dark wavy hair and was looking *mighty fine* in his suit.

"Check out number two," she muttered.

"Oh yeah!" MacKenzie replied.

But as the wedding party came closer, Erin's hopes evaporated. Number two was wearing a wedding band. Bummer.

The bridesmaids and groomsmen fanned out on either side of the pastor as the musicians paused, then started into the familiar *Wedding March.*

Erin couldn't suppress a squeal of delight when Nikki and her father arrived at the head of the aisle. Nikki's dress was ivory with a deep, V-neckline. The cap sleeves and fitted bodice were delicate lace that transitioned gradually into a flowing chiffon skirt. Her auburn hair was caught in a chignon at the base of her neck and covered by a veil edged in lace. She held a bouquet of creamy roses, accented with cranberry and pink flowers. Erin shot a glance at Darrin and was satisfied to see his mouth open and his eyes gleaming with tears as he gazed at his bride. Pure devotion. The way it *should* be.

After the appropriate dramatic pause, Nikki and her dad started forward, the leaves rustling and crunching under their feet. When she passed the row with the Camp Wallakee girls, Nikki grinned and shot them a wink.

The ceremony was surprisingly short and the pastor spoke only a few words of advice before leading the couple through their vows. Erin had expected something a bit more dramatic, but it appeared Nikki and Darrin were content with short and sweet. They hadn't even written their own vows.

After a long kiss, the beaming newlyweds turned to face the applause and cheers from the crowd.

"Ladies and gentlemen, Darrin and Dominique Pendleton," the pastor announced while Nikki and her groom shared another kiss. "The couple will greet guests here on the mausoleum steps, then there are docents available if you'd like a tour of the cemetery," the pastor continued. "If you prefer to skip the tour, there are cars waiting to take you directly to the Stratshire Club for cocktails and refreshments, then the reception will begin at six."

Erin and her friends joined the line that had quickly formed. When they reached Nikki, she squealed and held out her arms. "My Wallakee girls!"

For a minute there was chaos as everyone tried to hug and talk at once, but after a few minutes Nikki glanced at the line of guests waiting to greet her. "Listen, I'll see you at the reception, okay?" she smiled. "I put you all at the same table, so make sure to save me a spot."

They promised and after a final hug, they moved away as a group to the cemetery road.

"So what do you think?" Erin asked, eyeing the group of black-clad docents waiting for tour requests.

Taylor huffed. "No offense to Nikki, but I really don't want to traipse around a cemetery in these heels. I'd rather find some wine."

The rest of the girls agreed, so they piled into one of the waiting limos. Erin slid along the black leather seat to the front to make room for everyone.

"One down," she said in triumph.

"Almost two," Alyssa put in. "Holly's got her man."

"And Taylor," Lindsey added.

All eyes went to Taylor, who was staring fixedly out the window, even though the heavy tint made it hard to see much of anything. The unasked and unanswered question hung in the air. Does it count if you marry your billionaire, but then divorce him?

"Nikki looked so pretty," Erin said quickly. "I loved the way her hair looked with the ivory veil."

The girls launched into a conversation about the wedding, the dresses, the colors, the setting, and most especially, the groomsmen. Erin realized she wasn't the only one hoping Darrin had some wealthy friends. Though what were the chances they would all get to marry their dream man? The odds were pretty good someone was going to end up embarrassing themselves at their reception.

Her mind drifted back to the day they'd made the pact. It had been raining for three days and the camp was a quagmire of mud. After lunch, the counselors, evidently tired of cleaning up muddy footprints and trying to entertain scraggly groups of increasingly bored teenage girls, ordered everyone to their cabins with orders to *stay there.*

They played several rounds of UNO, Phase Ten, and Dominos, and Erin and Kynley did an impromptu talent show, but by dinnertime, everyone was bored and hungry.

Erin couldn't remember who came up with the idea of MASH (mansion, apartment, shack, house). Maryn handed out paper and they all listed four options for future dreams, including what kind of house they would have, who they would marry, where they would live, and how many children they would have. According to the rules, one of the options in each category had to be lame – like living in a shack, or ending up with two dozen children, or marrying a boy you couldn't stand.

One by one, they took turns picking a number and crossing off the corresponding items on their lists until they were down to one option each.

"This is dumb," someone, probably Holly, had finally said. "I'm definitely not going to live in a *shack*. My daddy says I'm going to marry a rich man and live in a mansion, end of story."

Erin had looked at Holly in awe. Aside from a few who attended on grants, the girls all came from affluent families – you had to be well off to afford Camp Wallakee – but the idea that you could *plan* to marry money, was new to her.

"Me too," Taylor had insisted.

"Let's all promise to marry rich guys," Erin said as inspiration struck. So the Billionaire Bride Pact was formed. They went around the room and each girl took her turn raising her hand and declaring, "I, _____, do solemnly swear that someday I'll marry a billionaire."

Lindsey drew up a contract and they all signed their names. As the years went by, they stayed in touch and eventually acknowledged that maybe *billionaires* was a little unrealistic. Nevertheless, they periodically reaffirmed their pledge to marry well.

And with Nikki's wedding, they were underway.

Read more or buy *The Passionate One* <u>here</u>.

54424104R00104

Made in the USA
Columbia, SC
30 March 2019